PEBBLE

Adventure of a Drone

PEBBLE

Adventure of a Drone

by
Jane McKay

PEBBLE
ADVENTURES OF A DRONE

ISBN: 978-0-578-66355-5 (Paperback Edition)
ISBN: 978-0-578-66356-2 (eBook Edition)

Printed in the United States of America.
Published by arrangement with IngramSpark
www.ingramspark.com

For my family,
For all their love and support.

*"To consider the Earth as the only populated world
in infinite space is as absurd
as to assert that in an entire field sown with millet,
only one grain will grow."*

— Metrodorus of Chios
4th century BCE

Prologue

It was small, as all of them were, and squeezed together by the thousands in a sphere-shaped delivery system. The worker could see hundreds, maybe thousands, of delivery structures in their launch bays as he looked down the huge enclosed space. The innovative system was three-prong, with a canon to launch the orbs into space, and at a fixed distance, the orbs would expel the small drones on their way. They loaded these spheres into the enormous canons that stood like soldiers waiting to go to war. This would be the last big effort to discover other worlds awaiting the spark of life in the surrounding galaxies. No answer had arrived from the other efforts sent out over the hundreds of years to find an available world to colonize.

I hope this effort is not too late, the volunteer thought. He and his world were running out of time. *I can only hope that if anybody gets one of these, they will know we existed.*

He peered toward where their star was entering its final phase. The inhabitants of his world had developed plans long ago when they first realized that their star was entering its last phase of life. The government and scientists had overseen the

1

massive project to save as many of the species on their planet as they could. They had previously sent all the inhabitants and breeding pairs of species into space in generational ships. He was one of many who had stepped forward to remain behind to do this one last task. He would not survive to see if his friends and relatives found a new home, but he was comforted knowing he had given all he could to aid in discovering a path to a new beginning.

"Let's get ready," a voice said as his companion halted behind him. He turned toward the man and clasped forearms with his new friend in a final goodbye. Volunteering for this last service had made them comrades as they faced death together.

"The view should be spectacular," his friend smiled in answer. "I'm grateful we had sufficient time to send our people away to locate a new home. Yes, let's get ready."

Together, they hustled into suits that would let them breathe long enough to complete this last stage as the sun ripped away the air. The ground heaved beneath their feet as they fought their way to the controls. They saluted the emblem of their world one last time as they launched the cannons to send the delivery systems on their way. It was the same emblem that was on the ships that now carried their hopes for their people.

As the delivery systems flew into the atmosphere, the solar wind of the dying sun caught them and sped them on their way. The men's fear melted away as they stood together watching the spheres shoot into space. Their last view was the vivid and majestic view of spheres flying outward in all directions. Holding onto each other, the two men fell; two of thousands of men and women who offered their lives for this moment. The planetary system that they had always known was being totally changed forever. Their star would consume the inner planets as it swelled in size. Once its fuel was gone, it would collapse into a dwarf star; no longer producing enough heat to warm the larger outer worlds that remained. Those worlds would continue to circle their faded star, but would gradually cool and freeze.

The spheres shot into space, unaware of the annihilation behind them. The solar wind from their ballooning sun drove them before it. Faster and faster, they accelerated in their race for the freedom of space. When they reached the predetermined distance from the dying planet, the spheres split open and their precious cargo of drones were projected outward. Each small drone sent out a signal detailing its position and direction. These signals, it was hoped, would be picked up by one of the many ships of survivors already speeding through the blackness. Some drones collided into one another and shattered, while some flew in pathways that would possibly take them back the way they came only to be incinerated in the solar wind. But a few flew true, destination unknown. The drones would last hundreds of years in the vastness of space. Because they couldn't navigate, some would travel into space debris and some would take up orbits around established planets. Cold, dead rogue planets traveling to far off destinations would even capture some, dragging the drones along to patrol their solitary way through the vastness of space. Other drones would feed hungry suns. But one flew for many years through the blackness of space, hoping to discover a suitable system with a planet in the correct zone to protect life. Finally, it entered a planetary system of relative newness with many planets, including gas giants, many asteroids, and some smaller rocky planets. Eventually, it spied a planet that piqued its curiosity the most. As it flew toward it, it noticed that the planet was predominantly blue, and the drone thought it was particularly nice looking. The drone didn't have navigational ability so it quickly sent a report out indicating its coordinates. Its speed caused it to drop through the sky swiftly where it landed on the side of a lush volcano. Its protective shell had helped it withstand the fiery entry and plunge through the layers of atmosphere and the jarring impact of landing. Nestled there, the small drone again sent its signal, hoping it would be picked up sometime in the future. It was not without intelligence and other capabilities, of course. Its makers wanted the drones to survive as long as possible, so they gave the little seekers advanced artificial intelligence. Space travel has so many dangers and travel and communications could take such a long time; the drones needed to be able to make judgments, have some limited maneuverability, and learn about their surroundings quickly. Performing as it had been designed, it automatically reported the length of rotation of the planet, the quantity of satellites it had, the size and number of other planets in the system, and the type of star that heated the surface.

And there the drone laid until one day it registered that the soil beneath was shaking and heating. Its outer shell protected it securely even as it registered the quickening action into its data banks. Over the following days it registered that the shaking was growing more persistent and the temperature of the ground was rising rapidly. As a drone it had restricted mobility, so it rolled to a different site and performed yet more investigations. These assessments included periodic scans of the sky, which it noted had turned a reddish tint. The shaking did not seem as marked in its new area, but the temperature of the ground continued to rise. Concerned for its continued safety, it moved to a third location, but found no improvement in conditions. Cautiously, it moved three more times, each time looking for a safer location. All of this movement led to the first actual decision it had ever made. It rolled back to the second location which had the lowest temperature of all of the sample sites, and there it waited.

It waited through many planetary rotations and noted the wild temperature fluctuations and the many long periods where shaking did not take place. The drone felt relief, amazement, and then bewilderment. It did not know that the makers had given it feelings. It sent off its findings in a communication, but this time it also had a question about what it was feeling. Were feelings normal or was something amiss with its programming? It did not get an answer, unfortunately, but it had not received one since it had started on its long journey many years ago.

The drone laid there for a long time and regularly sent its messages as it sought to understand the symptoms of the mountain. The makers had programmed into its data banks information on planetary formation, such as elevation, water, air, soil, and fire and how they interacted, including volcano activity. It applied this knowledge as it examined its surroundings day after day. It sensed that the neighboring mountains also shuddered, but not as hard as the one where it rested. It knew it did not have enough mobility to travel to those other elevations before the mountain exploded. Whatever took place, it would be in the midst of it all, so it continued to send its reports and continued to patiently wait.

Some days later, it noted that the soil below was heating tremendously, quickly reaching several hundred degrees. At the same time, the red tinge in the air had deepened, highlighting a new column of ash above the crown of the mountain. It also noted that the air tasted and smelled like sulfur. It sent off what it thought would be its last report and again waited. The shaking of the ground increased yet more, throwing the drone one way and another on the loosened soil, mostly downhill. Meanwhile, the temperature continued to soar higher and higher. A red swirling material it registered as magma started rolling out of the apex and travelled in cascades down the sides of the mountain, devouring the ground as it progressed. Gradually the magma caught up to the little drone as it was tossed back and forth and it wondered if its tough outer shell would continue to save it or if this would be its end.

The little drone rolled into a pocket of gas and the red-hot magma immediately surrounded it, gas and all. It bounced within the slippery gaseous prison down a sluice and eventually fell into a cold stream of mountain water that hissed and steamed. It didn't know it, but the magma slide and the sudden cold-water bath had just rescued it from dissolving under the strain. The rapid cooling of the magma caused a hard shell of solid rock to develop around the pocket of gas that had in turn imprisoned the small drone within it. The drone was amazed that it could function given the extremes it had been subjected to, but it also knew its reports would not be able to get through the magma crust that had developed around it. It lit its built-in light to see the interior of the stone that surrounded it. At first it saw only the swirl of gas, but over time it repeatedly checked its surroundings, and it saw gradual changes within the walls of its prison. It saw beautiful purple crystals form and the creations of rocky growths all around it. It thought for a long time and decided to record the state of its environment inside the little prison. It concluded that it could do nothing more until its circumstances changed, so it closed itself down to wait.

Years passed and mountains rose and fell. Flowers bloomed on mountainsides and in fertile fields, made rich with volcanic soil. Insects developed to forage on the flowers as the atmospheric oxygen increased, which aided in the development of new life-forms. Streams meandered and fell over falls into pools. The sun blessed the planet with its rays, which helped more plants to become prolific. The little drone continued to sleep on quietly, not aware of all the changes taking place around it or the passage of time.

Many species of animals and plants emerged and vanished in the centuries it slept. Finally, one species dominated where others had failed and died away. The drone knew nothing about that as it continued to sleep. Humans were now in charge.

Humankind developed cities and technology. People explored the planet, first on foot, later by horse and caravan, and eventually via cars, trains, and airplanes. In a curious habit, they collected souvenirs of where they had been when voyaging far from home. This led to whole communities being built in faraway places, and to the development of an industry that did nothing more than go around picking up objects off of the ground to provide for collectors and explorers. The drone slept through all this activity. Being so snugly encased, it took no notice of the changes made by the humans all around it. Not until one day...

Chapter One

Thomas Baumgardner, a tall, slender man, glared into the mirror of his renovated bathroom, as he knotted his tie and debated with himself about leaving on this business trip to Arizona. He just didn't want to go, but it was a trip with two extremely important meetings. He knew his boss, who was also going on this trip, would not appreciate him saying he preferred to remain home with his family. As the director of the department of Finance at Dianna Research he was responsible for signing off on this project, so he was required to go. He groaned in defeat as he looked in the mirror and realized he had to start over on his tie for the third time.

"Almost ready?" his wife, Colleen, asked from the doorway.

Tom glanced at his pretty wife and marveled anew how he got so lucky. She was a medium height woman at 5 foot, 5 inches tall, with medium length soft brown hair that she wore in a layered cut that waved around her head, and the biggest blue eyes he had ever seen, and she was the love of his life.

"Coming, as soon as I deal with this tie."

He was really mangling the tie, which was a shame because it was a wonderful mauve color and had been a Christmas present last year.

"You constantly have trouble with your tie when you don't want to go somewhere," she laughed as she drew the tie out of his hands and deftly tied it for him.

He laid his forehead on hers and caressed her arms. "Caught me again," he said.

Yes, he thought, *I'm sure lucky.*

"Don't worry, I kind of like to tie your tie. What's troubling you this time?"

"I worry about all of you, you know that, but this time Jenny is sick."

"The doctor says she'll be fine. She just has a case of the flu."

"I know, but after almost losing her when she was born, I suppose, I worry about everything." *Tom thought of the little baby Jenny had been when she had been born a month and a half early. She had been so tiny and helpless. Even Colleen, who had developed a kind of hypertension, called pre-eclampsia at the end of the pregnancy almost lost her life trying to bring their baby into the world. A C-section was done to ease the pressure on the baby while the physicians treated Colleen. Thank heaven they both got through that okay. They spent the ensuing months going through all the tests to determine if they had any remaining issues from Jenny coming so early. There were a few, but he and Colleen met each problem head on; and Jenny, today, was an active and healthy child. He still couldn't express his emotions from that time in his life. He didn't know where he would be today or what he would have done if anything had happened to either of them. Their families had been wonderful and supportive, but he still suffered from a fear of losing them.*

"Tom, she is a completely healthy, lively kid. She'll be fine. Come on, say goodbye or you'll miss your plane. Promise to call me from Phoenix when you get there."

He followed her down the hallway to Jenny's bedroom. It was a bright room with pale lavender walls and multi-colored pillows, animal pictures on her walls, family pictures scattered on the desk and shelves, and so many stuffed animals he had to watch his step as he crossed to the bedside.

"Hi pumpkin," he whispered as he bent over his seven-year-old daughter. "I need a kiss to last me till I get home again."

"I'll miss you, daddy. I'll make you cookies when you get home, okay?" She knew her daddy's love of cookies so well, she used it as a bribe to get him to come home as soon as possible.

"That's a deal I can't refuse." He eyed her and asked, "Chocolate chip?"

"Okay," Jenny said as she yawned.

He kissed her gently on the cheek as she closed her eyes in sleep, then said "I'll see if I can get you a geode to go with your collection."

He looked over to see her pretty collection of opened geodes with their myriad of colors and sizes. They ranged from tiny, barely an inch across up to five inches across. They looked very festive in Jenny's pretty bedroom. Sadness was the first reaction he had as he looked at her collection, for they revealed how often he had to leave for his job. He glanced down at his child and thanked God again for his family.

But Jenny was already asleep.

"At least it's a direct flight," said Colleen. "I was surprised they didn't do a conference call."

"It's a security issue. Thanks to whoever set up the direct flight. I really dislike flights that land at every airport between here and my destination. They take forever and invariably I have to switch planes, and the gate is always on the other side of the building." Tom grabbed Colleen, tickled her, and said, "Come here, my pretty."

"Tom, stop! Stop that now, you'll be late for your flight," she laughed as she backed away from him down the creamy yellow hallway. He noted she couldn't help grinning at the Wizard of Oz reference.

He grabbed her one last time and whispered, "miss me while I'm gone?"

"You know I will," she whispered back as he headed out the door.

Forty-five minutes later, Tom parked his car in long-term parking and ran into the terminal to see Jamarr Goode, his boss, waiting for him.

"You're late. They already announced our flight and if we don't hustle, they won't let us on the plane. Everything okay at home?"

"Jenny is sick, and I stopped to say goodbye." Tom informed him as they rushed down to the gate. They had to evade people and carts and more construction, which seemed to be everywhere. They got through security in record time and skidded to a halt at their gate with their boarding passes in hand.

"Oh perfect, we were going to close the door for your flight." The flight attendant said as he took their boarding passes and waved them through.

Both Jamarr and Tom gave a huge sigh of relief as they found their seats and stretched out their legs as much as they could. Tom, being taller, had a harder time getting comfortable.

"Too bad we can't get first-class tickets anymore; I miss the leg room. But I have to admit I like this better than sitting through a bunch of meetings," Jamarr murmured.

"Yep, me too." Tom replied as he closed his eyes.

Chapter Two

The drone continued to sleep on and off through the centuries, but it periodically sought to send a message, even though the basalt cage that held it would not let the signal through its hard shell. Gradually, it noticed that its area inside the shell had begun to transform. As groundwater seeped into the shell, the gas that was there blended with the moisture and began changing into crystals. The drone used its ability to generate a light to see its surroundings and it spun around in its little area, delighted to see the beautiful crystals and stalactites had grown inside the shell. The last time it had turned on its light, the crystals and stalactites were starting to develop. Now they were a beautiful blue and violet. It extended its sensors which revealed they were composed of micro-organisms multiplying in the groundwater soup that would gradually create a druse. The drone's area in the geode was receding rapidly and it wondered if it would become so tight it would not be able to move.

Meanwhile, the environment outside its shell had altered drastically, and the drone now rested on the surface of a dry lake bed where a volcano and a stream had previously dwelt. Soon the rock-filled lake bed attracted the scrutiny of a company that collected geodes and other rocks to sell. The man who operated the front loader made short work as the machine scooped up a broad area of sand, rocks and geodes and transferring them into an open bed truck. The drone registered the motion, but trapped in its cocoon, all it could it do was wait and speculate about what was taking place outside its protective shell. Soon the truck travelled to a nearby warehouse where machines quickly separated the geodes from the sand and quartz rocks. These they categorized according to size; with the rough quartz rocks going into huge rock tumblers to be polished. The round geode containing the drone was dumped into a large box to be sold to rock stores, zoos, and rock shows. It could feel the rock being moved and handled, sometimes roughly and sometimes more gently, but it couldn't tell what was happening to it. All it could do was wait and wonder what would happen next. It got used to being moved around and occasionally dropped, but nothing happened to damage or open its shell. It realized that something else was needed to open its prison from the outside.

One day everything changed. It was plucked up and put into something and carried. It didn't know where it was going, but it hoped that its shell would finally be opened.

—◈—

Tom became fascinated by the selection of items for sale in an interesting rock shop when he and his peers stopped for lunch in Sedona, Arizona, He took his time peering at all the items being presented and finally chose a delicate scarf in soft tones of blue which would match Colleen's eyes. When he stopped to peruse the bin of geodes, he was hard pressed to pick just one, but one piqued his interest. It was bigger than all the small ones, and it was heavier too. He also looked at the huge ones, but he wanted Jenny to have the fun of opening it herself, and the large ones tended to be solid crystal inside, and needed special equipment to open them. He recalled when that had happened before, Jenny had been really disappointed. At seven years of age, it was hard for her to understand that the solid crystal inside the geode had once been gas. That was the deciding factor in his mind. He wanted to see her face when she opened it to discover beautiful crystals. So, Tom carried the heavy geode to checkout.

"Excuse me, this one seems heavier than the others, is it a different type of geode? I thought there might be something different available and this one looks different somehow." He said with a smile.

"I'm sorry, sir, you will have to talk with the geologist who is not here right now. He's the store owner and he'll be back sometime tomorrow if you want to come back then. I don't know that much about the geodes myself," sales clerk said in an apologetic voice. "I'm sorry, but I don't see any difference. I do know this group of geodes came from a company that's near Flagstaff."

"I can't get here tomorrow because I'm actually passing through on my way to Flagstaff. Looks like we will just miss each other. Maybe I can call him if I get a chance. I'm getting

17

this for my daughter because she thinks she is an amateur geologist. Maybe it will be in one of her books. Oh wait, do you have a book on the volcanoes or geodes that formed in this area?"

"Yes, we do, here it is, I hope it can answer your questions. Okay, with the book your total is $97.45. I hope you have a safe trip," she added with a smile as she handed him his purchases.

He rushed out to the rental car where his co-workers waited. "I hope you got Colleen a gift too or you will never hear the end of it," Jamarr kidded him. Tom reached in the bag and drew out the beautiful scarf. Everyone burst out laughing. Jamarr rolled his eyes and said, "told you."

They arrived in Flagstaff near dinner time after a long, hot, aggravating ride in miles of highway construction. Their second business meeting was early the next morning, which allowed little time to plan and get some sleep. None of them were in a good frame of mind. The next morning, they met for breakfast downstairs in their hotel and had a brief discussion to go over the analysis of the financials before the meeting. The Dianna Research Institute, even though it was well endowed, still needed Tom to stay on top of the finances for this next important project. He needed a thorough working familiarity of the project so it wouldn't go over budget. Jamarr was in charge of the project, but Tom had the purse strings.

"Well, we survived so far, so we can get through this and go home. I say hear, hear to that." Jamarr smiled hesitantly, not being certain how everybody felt. Everyone grumbled, which Jamarr took as not a good sign. "Okay gentlemen, get it together. We need to do a good job in this meeting." This statement was met with a few dark looks.

"It's okay everyone, just do your best and we'll come out all right." Jamarr assured them, which helped remove a little of the strain. Later, after the lengthy meeting, they looked at one another and beamed in relief.

"Nailed it," Jamarr gave a high five to each task force member after the successful meeting. "Let's pack and go home." Jamarr and Tom were both relieved that the meeting had gone so well.

Before the airplane taxied out onto the runway, Tom called home. "On my way home," he told her as he stretched out. He was asleep before the plane passed the end of the runway and forgot all about the call to the owner of the rock shop.

Chapter Three

Tom couldn't wait to get home, and it meant a lot to him when he saw both Colleen and Jenny waiting for him when he got off the plane. The walk to baggage claim was full of hugs and smiles. His fellow workmates smiled and waved as they passed on their way to their cars.

"You are a lucky man," Jamarr told him as he headed out the door.

Colleen reached over and gave Tom an enormous hug. Surprised, Tom turned to her.

"What was that for? Did you miss me that much?"

"I'll tell you later," she gave his shoulder a squeeze and turned to wave goodbye to Jamarr.

Jenny wrapped herself around her father and gave him a huge grin. "I have a surprise for you at home. Want to guess?"

"Is it a new tie?" Tom wondered.

"No, silly," Jenny laughed. "You get two more guesses."

"Hmmm," Tom pondered. "Is it an oil change for the car? You know, I really need one of those."

"No! Not an oil change," Jenny began to look concerned.

"I know, you made me cookies. Oatmeal raisin, right?"

"Chocolate chip!" Jenny wailed.

"You made my favorite. Let's hurry and go home, I can't wait to eat one or two or three, or maybe four. They are my favorite, after all." He said as they got on the bus to long-term parking.

Colleen took his arm and told him, "maybe two or three, not four. Jenny and I want some too."

Jenny practically danced into the attractive red brick home; she was so excited. Tom dropped his bags by the front door and eagerly walked back to the kitchen. He grabbed two cookies and reached for one more, but both girls grabbed his arm. He rolled his eyes as he bit into the cookie. He grabbed his chest and pretended to faint in ecstasy, causing Colleen and Jenny to giggle.

"Wow, this cookie is great!"

"What did you get me, Daddy?" Jenny asked as she danced in place. "I made the cookies, like I promised. Mom said you told me you would get me a geode, but I had already fallen asleep. I'm sorry I didn't kiss you goodbye," Jenny babbled in her excitement as she danced around her father.

Tom pretended to think. "Hmmm, Colleen, did I say that? I don't recall."

Jenny's forward movement stopped as her face fell, and she looked ready to cry.

"Oh, pumpkin, would I forget you? Come on, help me unpack and I'll show you what I got you."

Jenny lent an eager hand to the unpacking and when it was all done stood quietly waiting. She couldn't figure out what her dad was doing because instead of unwrapping a geode, he got an old towel out of the rag bin and then moved to the garage to get a hammer. Next, he got a pan out of a cabinet. Then he carried everything outside. She watched him carefully as he lay the towel out inside the pan, then he laid the largest geode she had ever seen on top and enclosed it with the end of the towel.

"Here let me show you how it's done."

Tom took the hammer and held the geode in place with one hand, as he tapped at the top of the geode with the hammer. The hammer slipped down the side of the geode and hit his hand.

"Ouch, well, don't do that. That hurt," he said as he sucked his thumb. "My advice is NOT to hold the geode in place, just tap it gently."

Finally, he handed her the hammer.

"Tap gently with the hammer until you hear a crack. Not too hard now."

Jenny followed his directions and after several blows of the hammer she was rewarded for a sharp crack that made everyone jump at the sudden noise.

"Okay, let's look and see if it opened up." Tom said as he picked up an edge of the towel. He quickly put it down again after taking a quick glance. "Oh, oh," was all he said as he rolled his eyes to Colleen, giving her a wink that Jenny couldn't see, looking very forlorn. "I was afraid of this.'"

"What? what?" Jenny cried.

Tom carefully drew back the towel and there in the pan was the geode, but now in three pieces. The inside differed from all other geodes he had ever seen. It was a beautiful purplish color and had stalactites.

"Ohhhh!" Said Jenny and Colleen, staring at the sparkling crystals.

"Well, will you look at that? It's purple, but it's not an amethyst, and I have never seen stalactites inside a geode. I got a new book that may explain this. We'll look it up together," he said grinning at his daughter.

Jenny grabbed one section to look more closely at it, and suddenly a small purple rock-like pebble fell out and rolled across the floor. She grabbed for it, but it seemed to roll under her fingers. Tom also made a grab for it, but Colleen beat them to it as she picked it up.

"What have we here?" she asked as she squinted at the small object, shifting it back and forth in her hands. What she saw was a small rock, like a polished agate, that was all purple with a large pink area on one side.

Tom looked at her and asked, "How could it have gotten inside a closed geode and it even looks like it has been polished? Jenny, I think you have a truly strange type of geode."

Colleen handed it over to Jenny, but kept a curious eye on it.

"Maybe water could have worn it down before the magma trapped it," Colleen offered as an explanation.

"Yes, you are probably right," Tom admitted. He smiled at Jenny and said, "Well, you have a mystery to share with the kids at school. You have the pebble and don't forget about your geode, it's absolutely different too. Do you have a special place in your room you want to put the pieces?"

"Yes, the geode pieces can go on the shelf with my other geodes. I think I'll put the pebble on my desk so I can see it from my bed." And she ran off to her room to put the geode pieces away.

"That's an excellent idea. Now I want more cookies," he said with a twinkle in his eye and a cookie monster voice. Then she ran back to get her daddy his promised cookie and make sure he didn't eat all of them.

Tom, patting his stomach, agreed they were excellent cookies, and he again thanked his daughter as he carried her to see her geode sections and the little pebble in her room. There she pleaded with him to read a book to her. He had no defense against her soft voice, so he settled down to read. It wasn't long before both of them were asleep and the forgotten book was on the floor.

Colleen found them like that and gently covered them with a soft blanket.

Chapter 4

A few days later, while Jenny was asleep, the drone sent an update on its condition. It also inspected Jenny's room and recorded the routine of the family as far as it could see and hear. Later, after it sent its report, the drone wondered if any of its people would ever get it. It was an enormous universe out there and it had travelled a long time in space before it got to this world. It also had lain a long time on the surface of the planet after touching down.

The drone felt a sense of release to be out of the geode, even if the crystals were certainly attractive, it enjoyed being out of the geode because now it could see how the crystals sparkled in natural light all the time. Also, it had more freedom of movement to explore. Most of all, the small drone wanted to make regular reports again. It wondered if any of its reports had found their way to its people, but the possibility existed that its people could have come while it was in the geode for so long, and it would never know. The most important factor was, it hoped, was that they were not still seeking in the vastness of space for someplace to call home.

Jenny was asleep, so it decided to take advantage of time to examine her room. So far that was the only room it had seen; it also wanted to know its coordinates. It scanned the dimensions of the room, which were exactly twelve feet by twelve feet, and it then considered the arrangement of the furniture. The drone compared the room to artifacts in its memory banks and concluded it contained a bed, a desk, a dresser and a side table next to the bed, but they didn't seem to form out of the floor. Then, it cataloged what it took to be several electronic devices. It noted that Jenny used a device that she could talk into and hear others talking back to her. That was on the desk. Also, she had a machine that displayed pictures of other people talking and other things it didn't understand yet. She didn't talk to the object, and so it just noted that it set on the dresser. The side table had a light on it and there was one in the ceiling. The shelves that contained the geodes stood next to the closet. She also had an assortment of hats and ribbons on a chair, and hairpins and bows on a higher shelf of the shelf unit. The drone could tell what those were by comparing them to items in its database.

It took advantage of being able to listen and watch Jenny's reaction to what she saw on the device. It sought to associate the words it heard to what it saw, but for now, it could only record the programs. The programs were confusing; it saw creatures with horns on their heads and different-looking fish in a rainbow of colors. It was all too confusing, so instead it watched carefully to understand what and how Jenny used the items in her room. It didn't understand why Jenny and her family put something on over their skins but, the closet held a variety of clothing. It recalled when it first became aware, before it was launched into space, that everyone wore clothes, so maybe all biological beings needed clothes.

It wanted to see the other areas, but would have to wait until Jenny carried it there. It probably could roll off the desk, it considered, so it rolled to the edge and scanned the distance, but it seemed a long way down. Instead, it settled down to wait.

Usually when Jenny woke up, the first object she saw was the drone. The small pebble sized drone fascinated her. It differed from all of her other rocks in her collection. One thing was, it was so much heavier than her other pebbles. Then there was the position of the pinkish area that seemed to change, almost like an eye. It seemed to move when she was not looking straight at it. No matter how quickly she turned her head, it always seemed to look in the direction it had been looking before she turned her head. She decided she would take it with her to school today to show her friends.

She quickly got dressed and picked up the small drone and slid it into her pocket. They always served breakfast in the kitchen at the island, reserving the dining room table for dinner in the evening. She hopped up onto the stool and dug the pebble like stone out of her pocket.

Chapter 5

The drone quickly scanned the room and noted that it had considerably more open space than Jenny's room. The layout of the kitchen had three visible rooms surrounding it. The drone studied the furniture to see if it could figure out how those rooms were used. It quickly moved its scanner back to its original position when Jenny suddenly turned her head and looked intensely at it. She picked it up and looked closely at the scanner. The little drone was careful to keep very still and in its original position. She shrugged and put it down as her father came in to join her.

"Good morning, pumpkin. Ready for school?" he asked as he sat on the stool next to her.

"I guess," she said without enthusiasm. She again looked at the little drone.

"Daddy, where did you get my geode?"

"Well, let's see if I can recall. I purchased it in Sedona, which is in Arizona."

"Where is Arizona?"

Her question reminded him that she was just 7 years-old and had not seen many maps. "Wait a minute, let me get something that might help." He dashed out to his office and grabbed an atlas. He opened it to a map of the United States. "Okay, here we go. I'll show you where we live first. This is a picture of what the world looks like from the air above us. Now we live in Columbus, Ohio, and that's here." He marked a red mark on the map. "I went to my meetings in two cities in Arizona, here in Phoenix and here in Flagstaff." He put a red mark on the two cities. "But we stopped in Sedona to get your and your mom's gifts." He then marked Sedona in red. "Does that help?"

"So, my geode came from Sedona?" she asked.

"That's right. At least, that's where I bought it."

"But Dad, where did the store get it and how did the pebble get inside?"

"Well, I don't know exactly where the geode formed. Dr. Malinda Gold is head of our Geology department at work, I can ask her to look at it. Maybe she can figure out where it came from."

"That would be great," she jumped down from her stool and gave him a huge kiss. "Oh, here it is in my pocket. I was going to take it to school and show my friends, but I really want to know where it came from. Can you do it today?"

"If she comes in, I'll ask her. I promise," he said as he smiled at Colleen over Jenny's shoulder.

Jenny handed her dad the pebble and grabbed her books and lunch as she dashed out the door to her school bus.

"I wonder why she is so interested in where the geode came from?" he said as he looked closely at the small drone.

Colleen set Tom's breakfast in front of him and waited for his reaction. He was so preoccupied looking at the pebble she had to move his breakfast a little closer. Only then did he look up at her. She again shifted the plate toward him. Finally, he looked down in puzzlement. There on his plate was the usual bacon, two fried eggs, and a piece of toast with butter and jelly. In the middle of his food was a small plastic baby. It took him a minute, but enlightenment dawned.

"Are you? Really? Pregnant?" he stammered. Colleen nodded her head with tears in her eyes as Tom staggered out of his chair to grab her and hold her tight. His own tears welled up and threatened to overwhelm him.

"Oh, Colleen, we'd hoped for so long. Are you sure? When did you see the doctor? What did the doctor say? Do you want to sit down? Are you feeling all right?" Words tumbled out, and he felt suddenly shy and protective of her. He wanted to wrap her in soft blankets and never let her out of his sight. "Oh, Colleen..."

She took his face in her hands and gently wiped his tears. Laughing, she said, "Oh I love you, Tom. We're having another baby. What a blessing!" She laid her head on his shoulder as she thought about the years since they had Jenny and how much they wanted another child. Not just to be a playmate to Jenny, but to enrich all their lives. Their prayers had been answered, and she was, as she was sure Tom was, so grateful.

The drone witnessed the two people and though it didn't understand what they were saying, it could scan them and analyze their physical responses to what they were saying. It thrilled the drone to see more of this world, and wondered if it could use its limited mobility to get around more. Unfortunately, Tom put it in his breast pocket and again it couldn't see anything. It scanned Tom's pocket and recorded all the sounds and smells it heard. His shirt smelled nice and was very soft. Also, it heard a noise like when it could hear rocks falling when it was in the geode. It didn't know what made the sounds, but it made a recording and maybe it could match it up later with other sounds to learn what have made them. It had a regular rhythm to it, and it wondered what it was.

The first thing Tom did when he got to his office was to call to see if Dr. Malinda Gold was in her office.

She greeted him through video chat with a smile and a coffee salute. "Well, hello Tom. What can I do for you this fine morning?"

"Well, I have this pebble that fell out of a geode I got my daughter when I was on my trip to Arizona, and my daughter wants to know where it came from. I got the geode at a great little rock shop in Sedona, Arizona., and …" Tom trailed off when he looked at her face.

"It fell out of the geode?"

"Yes."

"Can you bring it in so I can see it?"

"Sure, I have it with me. I'll be there in a minute or I can show it to you now," he said.

She thought for a minute and told him it would be better if she could see it and handle it. Malinda looked up in surprise as he came through her door a few minutes later. He gently gave her the small stone.

"It's a lovely pebble, and it is a little heavy," she said as she weighed it in her hand.

"It looks like a polished agate, but it can be from anywhere because polished agates are very common. I'm sorry Tom, but I can't help you any further than that."

"You can't?" he asked, astonished and disappointed.

"Don't look so stunned. I just need the geode itself so I can place how old it is and what it's made from. You see, there are many types of geodes and different substances that form them. I can probably track it from a piece of the geode itself and maybe even tell the volcanic field where it formed. Can you bring in the geode tomorrow and I'll see if I can detect where it came from?"

"I'll do that, hey, thanks for the help."

Tom moved back to his office and since he had the pebble in his hand, he laid it on his desk. The drone was very careful to keep its scanner looking in one direction. It scanned in the direction it was facing and recorded everything in that space. Tom's office was a glass enclosure with the desk facing the door, a couch and a couple of chairs. It recorded the activity it could see across the hallway and all the people wandering back and forth in the hallway. Tom played with the pebble as he talked on the phone with Jamarr about a virtual meeting that was coming up in two weeks.

Two days later, Jenny set out to research information about her pebble. The Geologist at Dianna Research was busy trying to track down which volcano formed the geode. Her dad had taken the pieces of broken geode to her, and was looking into its chemical signature, her dad said this meant that geologist could tell what area it came from, and maybe even identify which volcano it came from too. Jenny wasn't sure what the word 'chemical signature' meant. She decided she would ask her parents later. Jenny was excited about the geode but still puzzled by the pebble. It fell out of the geode and it seemed to move on its own. What did that? A pebble couldn't move on its own. And how did it get into the geode, anyway? Her dad told her some geodes formed thousands of years ago. Maybe some geodes form now, or maybe they form all the time.

Daddy will be home soon and then maybe he'll know which area my geode came from, she thought.

First, she looked at the book her teacher loaned her from school. She found it in the stack of books in her room. The pictures in the school book immediately attracted her, even though she couldn't read that well yet. She didn't see any geodes that looked like hers. Maybe her mom could help her with this book and the one her dad brought home from his trip.

"Mom… Mom," she yelled. "Where are you?"

"What, what's wrong?" Colleen called from the basement where she was doing laundry.

"Nothing's wrong. I just wondered if you could read this for me?" Jenny carried the book downstairs to Colleen so she could see what she was pointing out.

"Jenny, Mommy is doing laundry, can't this wait?"

"I suppose so, sorry." Jenny turned from her and walked dejectedly up the steps.

"Oh baby, I'm sorry. The laundry can wait a while. Of course, we can look at it together. Let's go into the kitchen."

"Okay," Jenny replied as she scampered away from her.

Colleen had the feeling she had just been played by her 7-year-old daughter. Shaking her head, she followed Jenny into the kitchen. For the next hour, they poured over the book with Colleen becoming as fascinated as Jenny. To get more comfortable, they moved into the family room and curled up on the couch. Colleen and Jenny were reading intently by the time Tom came home.

The last thing Tom expected was to come home and discover his two girls snuggled up on the couch reading a book.

"Well, hi there. Having a good time?"

They both yelled at the same time and jumped off the couch to rush into his arms, laughing.

"Wow," he thought, "a guy should get that kind of greeting every night."

Smiling, he drew them in his arms. "Love the greeting, but what's going on?" he asked.

"Jenny was showing me the most wonderful book you got her on your trip that's all about geodes. We were looking at all the books." Colleen told him with a wave of her hand toward the nearby pile of books.

"Did you talk to Doctor, er, Doctor, you know, the geologist?" Jenny asked quickly.

"Her name is Dr. Malinda Gold, and yes, I did, so why don't we sit down and I'll tell you what she said." Once they were settled, he continued, "well, it was a funny thing, really. I gave her the geode and in one look she told me she knew exactly where it was from and when it formed. She said it was from San Francisco Mountain volcano range that spans from Southern California, all the way to include all of Arizona and has about 550 volcanoes. The volcano formed the geode about 10,000 years ago. It's still considered an active volcano and it's located right there at Flagstaff, Arizona. The San Francisco Mountain Volcano is one of three still active volcanoes in Arizona that exploded many times in the past 5 to 16 million years, but the last eruption was about 10,000 years ago. So, the geodes from that eruption were probably the ones on top of the sandy lake bed. Cool."

"What are the names of the other volcanoes, Daddy?"

"Well, they are Uinkaret, Pinacate, and San Francisco Mountain. Are they in your book?" he asked. That had both Colleen and Jenny flipping pages once again. Tom joined them and together they read more about volcanoes, their types and locations. "Wow, look here, it claims that the state of Arizona has thousands of ancient volcanoes."

"Well, I, for one, am glad that we are safe, here in good Ohio. No volcanoes, ancient or active, here. At least, I hope," Colleen said as she looked up from the book.

"I wonder, let's look it up. Who knows, we might live on an ancient volcano right now," Tom wondered. That set both

Colleen and Jenny off on another search that kept them busy for a few minutes.

Tom wanted to share the wonderful news about the baby with Jenny, so he tugged Colleen's hair to get her attention. He whispered, "want to tell her about the baby?"

Colleen nodded.

"Jenny, we have something we want to share with you," Tom started.

Jenny looked up expectantly and Tom stammered to a halt. Colleen rolled her eyes and said, "Jenny, we're going to have another baby."

Jenny looked at them stunned. "Both of you?"

Tom and Colleen broke out laughing. "No, no, sweetheart. I'm afraid we are not doing a good job of telling you. You will have a new brother or sister soon," Tom explained.

Colleen took over for Tom. "I'm pregnant which means I have a baby growing inside me and in a few months the baby will be born and we will be a family of four, instead of three."

"So, Daddy is not growing a baby inside him too?" Jenny asked, trying hard to understand.

"No, only mommies grow babies inside their bodies," Colleen explained.

"Oh, okay," Jenny answered matter-of-factly as she grabbed her book and ran out of the room.

"Do you think she really understands?" Tom asked, concerned.

"Don't worry. She will soon enough," Colleen laughed.

Chapter 6

Every day seemed the same to the little drone. Colleen, Jenny's mother, generally had the TV on most of the day, even if she wasn't really watching it. She was always cleaning or running the vacuum which, it saw picked up dust and made a lot of noise. Since they had put the drone on the end table days ago, it had taken every chance it could to decipher what was being said or done around the house. The little drone couldn't tell what was real or not real when it looked at the pictures on the TV. It tried to compare what it saw with what was in its database of information.

Every day, it noted that Colleen went into the window-lined room off the kitchen. There she did all kinds of projects. The drone didn't understand what the projects were, but Colleen really enjoyed making them and wrapping them in brown paper. She then gave them to a man who came to the door. The little drone, being curious, hoped to scan that room soon.

One task that was programmed into the drone data storage unit was to automatically check any living beings around it, so it had already scanned Jenny, Tom, and the geologist. Now it had a chance to scan Colleen. It swiveled its scanner around so it could get a scan of Colleen. The drone made a full scan of Colleen and noted the differences between her and Tom. It also looked inside her in order to compare these scans with scans of the beings from its planet of origin. What surprised it was that they were very similar in appearance. The beings from its planet, called Maveners after the planet Maven, were also bipedal, though they had six digits on their hands and a reticulating membrane in their eyes. None of the people it had scanned so far had that membrane or the extra digit on their hands. They also had slight differences in the shape of their vocal cords and some of their organs. The species on this planet only had one heart, but had a lot of redundancy in other organs, like two lungs, and two kidneys. Maveners had one large lung with three lobes, and two hearts.

It froze in place when it noticed that Colleen was watching it. Colleen watched it for several moments, shook her head and went back to watching her program.

The drone noted movement in a small bowl of liquid on a table by the wall. It turned its scanner in that direction. The drone was excited because this was the first new life-form it had seen. Again, it noted movement inside the bowl. As it watched, a small biological creature drifted into view. The drone quickly scanned it. It was a perch latch, that was the word for it on its home planet, but the drone didn't know what they called it on this planet. The perch latch was one more similarity between its world and this one.

Suddenly, Colleen snatched the drone and peered intensely at it. Startled, it automatically emitted an intense flash of light and scanned Colleen eyeball.

"What the heck?" yelled Colleen as she dropped the drone to the floor. It took advantage to roll itself under the table. "Come back here." Colleen felt the carpet under the table, trying to locate the small drone by feel. It rolled this way and that, dodging her hand until it had rolled up against the wall. When Colleen got angrily to her feet, she hit her head on the table, and rubbing her head she went to get something she could use to get the little pebble out from under the table. It took advantage of her being out of the room to roll out from under the table to roll over under the couch.

She came back with a broom and got down on her knees to try and get the drone. The drone could see all of her from its hiding place under the couch, so it took advantage of that position to scan her again. Then it compared the two scans. It was interesting to see that her blood pressure had risen, her sweat glands were working harder, so she was sweating, and she had become agitated.

"There you are," Colleen cried in triumph as she scooped the drone up into a pan. "Let me look at you," Colleen said as she took it into the kitchen and placed it in a small bowl on the table. "I could swear you moved, or at least that eye thing moved, and what's with that light? Well, we'll see about that." She got up and got her camera, and then she got a small tripod out of a cabinet in her craft room. She spent some time putting the two items together. Finally, she arranged them so she could photograph the interior of the bowl where the little drone laid. All this fascinated the drone and it scanned the camera and tripod. She turned the camera on and walked back into the other room. "Let me see you get out of that," She said in exasperation, pushing her hair out of her eyes.

The drone watched her leave and then turned back to the camera. It scanned it again and noted that parts of the camera were now running. It pondered the camera's purpose. The drone wondered if it could get out of the bowl or was that something it shouldn't do, but being in the bowl made it feel like it was back inside the geode. It trembled with the sudden need to escape.

Colleen watched the pebble out of the corner of her eye. She still didn't know what that light was or why she thought she had seen it roll under the table, not under the couch. It came out of a geode, which had turned out to be a regular geode, but nothing could explain how it came to be inside that geode, which was thousands of years old.

Wait, did it move? Colleen wondered to herself and she watched closely to see if it happened again.

The drone didn't know what to do. It didn't know if it could get out of the dish by hopping. It looked in Colleen's direction to see if she was looking, but it looked like the program on the television engrossed her. The small drone gathered itself and struggled to hop. All it managed was a slight roll. He peeked again toward Colleen and was startled to see she was watching it.

Colleen jumped up and started toward the kitchen when her phone rang. She hesitated. The persistent ring won out, and she changed direction to answer the phone.

"Hello," She answered, her voice sounding stressed even to her own ears.

"Hello, Colleen? Is that you?" Nance's voice inquired.

"Oh, hi Nance. Yes, it's me."

"Oh, okay. It just didn't sound like you. Everything okay?"

"Yes, didn't mean to worry you. You just caught me when I dropped something important." Colleen looked again at the pebble.

"Oh, okay. I just wanted to let you know that we switched the time of the dinner party to 6 p.m. I hope that won't inconvenience you and Tom."

"No, that will be fine. Thanks for calling and letting us know. Sorry I snapped at you."

"No honey, it's fine. I'm just glad everything is okay. Bye now," Nance assured her.

Colleen hung up and turned to stare into the kitchen. The small stone still laid in the dish, but was now in a different spot. *Hmmm,* thought Colleen, *maybe I can just leave it there. The camera is filming, so if it moves the camera will catch it. Also, if it could hop out of that dish, it would have done it.*

Colleen glanced at the clock and realized that Jenny was expected home in a few minutes. She considered moving the dish and the stone somewhere else, but Jenny would just ask for her Pebble, which was her nickname for the small rock, so she left it there, and she would try to explain what she thought she saw.

Jenny came in the door full of questions, but before she could ask them, she saw the small rock sitting in the dish.

"Why is Pebble in a dish?" She made a move to pick it up and suddenly jumped back when her mother yelled out, "No!" Jenny jumped backward and looked in surprise at her mother.

"Why?" she demanded.

"I think I saw Pebble move. I know that sounds crazy, but I thought that if I recorded it trying to get out of the dish, I could prove it."

Jenny stared at her mom. "Mommy, I saw Pebble move the other day."

"Really? You too?" Colleen exclaimed, relieved that she hadn't imagined it.

Jenny nodded.

"Well, then I think we will leave it there and see if it moves." Colleen and Jenny both turned to look at the little pebble. After a minute, Colleen turned to Jenny and asked if she had any homework, Jenny shook her head no. "Well in that case, let's set the table. It will be strange having Pebble on the table, not to mention a camera and tripod, but we need to watch it. Can you get the tableware, please, honey?"

Together they got the table set and started preparing dinner. Tom came home to discover his girls staring at Pebble, who was sitting in a dish on the dining table. He wondered if he should ask or just wait. He decided to just wait and see what this was all about.

It was a notably quiet meal. Still Tom waited. He too, found himself watching Pebble in the dish and wondering what was happening. Soon the meal was over and everyone was helping to wash up the dirty dishes. Pebble laid quietly in the dish. Tom reached toward the dish, but both Colleen and Jenny shook their heads no, so he withdrew his hand, and with his eyebrows raised in question, retreated to the couch in the living room. He could still see the dish, and like Colleen and Jenny, he sat and watched the dish to see what would take place.

Colleen and Jenny curled up together on the couch. Tom, on the other hand, didn't know what was going on, so he stationed himself between the kitchen and his girls. If there was a threat, he didn't want it affecting them. Tom was soon grinding his teeth in frustration. He didn't know what was going on, but he wanted to know what it was.

Out of the corner of his eye, he thought he saw movement. He jerked in his seat, but Colleen laid a hand on his arm and squeezed. He turned and saw that both Colleen and Jenny were attentively watching the dish.

In a flash, Pebble was outside the dish and rolling toward the edge of the island. Tom jerked out of his chair, but Colleen and Jenny were quicker. They dashed into the kitchen in time to see Pebble scurry under the refrigerator. Colleen grabbed her broom and Jenny had her butterfly net she got last year for Christmas. They took up positions on either side of the appliance and waited. Tom looked on in astonishment as they did a perfect pincher movement to catch the small stone.

47

Suddenly Tom yelled, "What the...?" just as Pebble rolled, bashing into his two feet. He took a towel and threw it over the stone. All three of them pounced on it as the towel moved swiftly across the floor. Tom felt over the top of the towel until he spotted the small mound in the middle. He gathered it up in the towel and stepped toward the dish. Colleen quickly stopped him from placing the pebble back in the small dish. She reached into the cabinet and produced a large mixing bowl, this she put in place of the small dish. Tom carefully placed the towel in the large bowl and exposed the pebble.

Pebble sat absolutely still. Tom looked at the pebble and the pebble looked at Tom. Colleen and Jenny crowded close to gawk at the pebble. The pebble started to vibrate and Tom, Colleen and Jenny stepped back in fear, not certain if something dangerous would happen. Tom stepped in front of Colleen and Jenny, wanting to protect them from anything that happened.

Jenny suddenly dashed around Tom and exclaimed in understanding.

"It's frightened. Mom, look, it's shivering."

And before Tom or Colleen could intercept her, she picked up the little pebble and rubbed it against her cheek, murmuring to it that everything was all right.

Tom and Colleen both reached out to her, but the pebble wriggled against her cheek and emitted a purring sound, so like a cat, that all three of them instinctively smiled.

"That settles that, the thing is alive. Okay, Jenny put it back in the bowl," Tom told her. "Let's see if it can communicate."

"Maybe we can ask it questions first," Colleen said and turned to the small stone. "Pebble, do you know your name?"

Pebble recognized what Jenny always called it. It wasn't sure what else Colleen said, so it made a small sound. Colleen smiled in triumph.

"Can you talk? I mean can you speak?" Tom asked.

Pebble emitted a string of beeps and squawks and looked at all of them.

"That sounds a lot like a computer. Could it be like a binary language? That's like a universal vocabulary that people use to create programs for computers," Tom explained to Jenny. "I have a beginner's programming textbook. Let me get it." Tom wondered if that would work, but he ran to his office to look for the book.

Pebble turned to Colleen and emitted a small sound. Colleen shrugged in answer as she glared at the rock.

"Let's see what I can find," he said as he came back with the book in hand. "Ok, let's try this."

Pointing at himself, he wrote 01010100 for T, 01101111 for O, and 01101101 for M. He slowly said the sound for each letter and then he pronounced his name and again pointed to himself.

Pebble looked at the binary code for T o m and became very excited.

Tom pointed at Colleen and wrote 01000011 for C, 01101111for O, 01101100 for L, 01101100 for another L, 01100101 for E, 01100101 for the second E, and 01101110 for an N. Again, he told Pebble the sound for each letter and said the name while pointing at Colleen.

Pebble looked at the code and then turned to Colleen. Tom was very excited by his success so far.

Tom pointed at Jenny and wrote 001001010 for J, 01100101 for E, 01101110 for N, 01101110 for N, 01111001 for Y. Again, he repeated the same process.

Pebble turned to Jenny. The whole family was laughing, and Jenny picked up Pebble and rubbed it against her cheek. Again, Pebble emitted the purr.

Tom pointed to Pebble and wrote 01010000, 01100101, 01100010, 01100010, 01101100, 01100101 which translated to P E B B L E.

Pebble again purred and snuggled into Jenny's cheek. "Je…" Pebble tried to speak. It struggled to correlate the sounds it heard with the programmed binary code on which it based its vocabulary.

The whole family beamed at it. Tom quickly wrote 01011001, 01100101, 01100011 and quickly nodded his head to let Pebble know the word was 'Yes.'

It was a beginning, and the whole family hoped that normal communication would be possible in a few days of working with Pebble. Pebble kept trying to say Jenny's name, and every try got it a hug from her.

Tom wondered if Pebble had an interface that could connect with his computer.

"Let me try an idea, I'll be back in a moment."

He raced to his office and grabbed his old laptop and came rushing back to put it on the table. He opened it up and started the computer. Pebble watched and then rolled over and all around the outside of the laptop. An arm on Pebble popped out, and it tried to put it in one of the USB ports. It wouldn't go in and Tom deflated. He hadn't realized he had been holding his breath. Pebble again moved around the laptop. This time it popped out a different arm from its side and inserted it in one port. This time it went in and suddenly the computer went crazy. Pebble was flipping through files and firewalls at lightning speed. Tom quickly tried to recall what he had on that laptop, but then he remembered he had put that laptop aside when he got his classified job so no questionable information was on this laptop. *Whew,* he thought. In his haste to get a way to communicate with Pebble, he almost compromised security.

Pebble gorged itself on vocabulary and ideas and anything else it could find. It took about an hour for it to download all the information on the computer. The family had watched for the first fifteen minutes, but Pebble was still downloading. They drifted off one by one to do other tasks. Tom went to his office to say a prayer of thanks he had not grabbed the wrong laptop, and to wonder what questions Pebble could answer when the download was completed. Colleen went to review their bills and to do other tasks around the house, and Jenny went to play games on her lap pad. Tom heard his name, but it didn't sound like either Colleen or Jenny's voices.

"What... who?"

He went to investigate the new sound. He was very startled to find Pebble turning in circles while it named items in the room. It also kept saying Tom's, Colleen's and Jenny's names over and over. In between saying each of their names, it would utter a purr. As Tom came into the room, Pebble launched itself right into his arms.

"Tom, Tom, Tom." it repeated as Tom cradled it in his hands. Colleen and Jenny came dashed into the room next, and Pebble started shouting their names over and over. Tom had trouble holding onto it.

"Pebble!" exclaimed Jenny as she dashed up to her dad.

"Jenny!" cried Pebble as it launched itself neatly into Jenny's arms. It purred loudly.

"Daddy, Daddy, my friends will love Pebble, can I take it to school now?" Jenny danced around in excitement.

Tom and Colleen exchanged looks.

"Sweetheart," Colleen said in her soft voice.

"Daddy, please?" she said as tears welled up in her eyes.

"Daddy has to make sure it's okay first. Let me find out and if it is okay, then you can take it to school. Okay? Promise?" Tom asked her.

"Okay, I promise."

Colleen moaned. "We missed the party at Nance's. She called to tell me she had switched the time to six o'clock. I forgot all about it."

Tom laughed. "Call her now and apologize. Just tell her we had a mouse in the kitchen or something like that."

"Don't forget tomorrow we're going to the game," she called to him as she went down the hallway to the phone.

"Oh, and don't forget to confirm with Annette about sitting. Game starts at 3:30pm, so we have to leave at noon." Tom worried about what Pebble might do or say in front of the sitter while they were gone, so he resolved that he needed to have a talk with both Jenny and Pebble first. He went searching for them and found them together in Jenny's bedroom.

"Daddy, look at what I made!" Jenny had made a nest for Pebble to rest in at night when she was asleep. She had put it right across the room from her bed so she could see it anytime she opened her eyes.

"Hey pumpkin, that's great," he said, then jumped when Pebble launched itself into his hands. He automatically started to pet it like he was petting a cat, but suddenly stopped when he realized what he was doing. He passed it to Jenny. "Hey, you two. I need you to listen now. Tomorrow, your mom and I are going to the game and you will have Annette here. It is very important that you don't let her know that Pebble can talk. Okay? You don't want to scare her; she's probably not used to talking rocks."

Jenny listened carefully to her father and then looked at Pebble.

"Can Pebble just stay in my pocket?"

"How about Pebble stays in that nice nest you made? We'll be home right after the game, and then we can talk with Pebble. Would that be okay?"

"I guess so," said Jenny dejectedly.

The next day, promptly at noon, the next-door neighbor, Annette Cunningham, showed up at the door. She was staying at her daughter's house while they were on a cruise, and Jenny seemed to like her.

"We will only be gone a few hours," Colleen told her. She had fixed a lunch for them and had purchased a couple of movies for them to enjoy while they were gone. She and Tom probably would be home before they had finished them.

"You have our cellphone numbers if you need us, right?" Colleen asked Annette as she put on her OSU earrings.

"Yes, Jenny will be fine, Colleen. Have a good time," Annette assured her.

Tom smiled at Annette as he pulled a strand of the team's colored beads over his head. Tom and Colleen left for the game in high spirits and loaded down with seat cushions, packed lunches and drinks that they could have when they parked in the college parking lot before the game.

"After lunch, let's go walk around a little before we go to our seats," Tom suggested as they headed toward the car.

"Sounds wonderful. It's a good day for the game. It's not chilly and it's not raining. How did we get so lucky?" Colleen joked.

Meanwhile, back in the house, Annette told Jenny, "You go ahead and start your lunch and I'll join you as soon as I turn on the TV for you." Annette moved into the TV room to look at the movies and turn on the set.

"Do you have a favorite movie you want to see?" Annette asked her. Jenny said no.

Jenny went into the kitchen and started eating the lunch her mom had made. She watched Annette as she devoured her lunch. Jenny hoped Annette would be a smiling and fun person who joked and played with her. This was different somehow; Annette was fussing around the room, so Jenny decided that she would get Pebble to keep her company, so she went to her bedroom and picked up Pebble to put into her pocket.

"What's that?" asked Annette from the doorway.

Jenny jumped in surprise and dropped Pebble on the floor. Pebble remembered what Tom and Colleen had said about not letting the sitter see it, so it stayed very still as the sitter bent to pick it up.

"It's beautiful," Annette mused as she looked at its colors. "Well, I have the TV up and running so come along and watch a movie if you are done eating."

Annette moved back to the TV room, still carrying Pebble.

"Come now, Jenny, the TV is on." Annette called as she got her lunch. She looked out the door to see if Jenny had heard her.

When Jenny joined her, she saw that Annette had picked her movie for her, so she sat on the couch and watched. Jenny was so bored.

"Jenny, I'm sorry, I forgot I still had your rock in my pocket. Here you are," she said, handing Pebble back to the girl. "Don't you like the movie? Or do you want to see a different one?"

"It's okay," she slumped further into her chair.

Pebble also watched and tried to analyze what the sitter was doing. Annette had brought her crocheted sweater to work on while Jenny watched TV.

"Can I go outside to play?" asked Jenny in a disgruntled voice.

"It is a very nice day today. I think that might do us both some good." Annette agreed as she gathered up her crochet items. "I can do this on the porch while you play."

They both happily moved outside and Jenny had fun tossing Pebble up in the air and catching it. Neither one saw the three older kids riding their bikes quickly down the sidewalk. They came riding over flowers and in-and-out between parked cars. In other words, they were a danger to themselves and others.

"Gotcha!!" yelled one as he snatched Pebble out of the air and threw it across the street.

Annette yelled at the boys, but it was too late. Jenny had dashed after Pebble without looking.

The boys speeded on down the sidewalk, laughing. Only the squeal of tires had them looking back.

A panicked Jenny had chased after Pebble, running across the street without looking. A startled car driver coming down the street quickly slammed on her brakes; her relief at seeing that Jenny was okay caused her to put her head down to slow her racing heart.

Annette hurried to the driver, "Are you okay?" she checked to see if the driver had hit her head with such a hard stop and received a nod, then she continued across the street.

"Jenny, are you okay? Let me look at you," Annette said, anxiously checking Jenny for injury.

Jenny grabbed Pebble a second before she was lifted into Annette's arms and brought back to her house

Jenny said in a small voice, "Those boys threw Pebble across the street and I went to get it. I'm sorry, I forgot to look both ways."

"What the boys did was wrong. You could have been hurt or that kind lady driving the car could have hit her head when she stopped so quickly. But you both are okay, so now I think, we should go in and watch a movie and you can introduce me to your little friend you are holding so tight. It keeps rolling its eye at you and purring."

Jenny looked down at Pebbles and sighed, then she introduced it to Annette. Annette wasn't at all disturbed by a talking rock and they all exchanged information about their lives. Annette talked about her daughter and son-in-law, Jenny told how Pebble had rolled out of a geode her daddy had bought for her, and Pebble talked about its journey to Earth.

Then they settled down to watch a movie, all three of them in front of the TV - Annette, Jenny and Pebble.

Chapter 7

Colleen couldn't sleep, so she reluctantly got out of bed. She wasn't sure what had woken her, but now that she was up, she wanted to do something she had not had time for the last few days. She would paint. On her way to her craft room, she passed Jenny's room, so she stopped to check on her. A few moments later, she was so glad she did. Jenny was asleep and, on her palm, Pebble laid resting too. Pebble's pink eye rotated around to look at Colleen, who put her finger to her lips and softly whispered, "shh." She got her camera and took a photograph, and then after getting a cup of coffee, went into her studio off the kitchen. There she got her sketching materials and made a drawing of Pebble and Jenny sleeping together. She worked steadily, transferring her design to watercolor paper, and soon had a working piece. She was so absorbed she didn't realize what time it was until Tom surprised her when he put his arms around her. He looked at the painting and caught his breath. She had captured perfectly the sense of trust between Jenny and little Pebble.

"It's beautiful," he whispered to her.

"Yes, it is. Oh, Tom, it's like it was meant to be. I don't know how to explain it."

"I know, I know. I feel it too."

Pebble rolled across the room and then hopped on a table next to the watercolor. Tom and Colleen both turned when they heard it land on the table. Pebble stared at the painting and turned to look at both Tom and Colleen.

"I love Jenny," it said.

"Yes, I believe you do. Jenny loves Pebble too," Colleen said.

"I can take a picture too," and a bright flash went off, startling Tom and Colleen. "I took a picture of you both. Tom loves Colleen."

"Well, now I know where that flash came from when I first met you." Colleen commented as she blinked her eyes.

"Yes, that explains a lot," Tom laughed, causing Colleen to grin in response.

Pebble surprised Colleen by hopping up into her hands. It rubbed against her cheek and purred very loudly.

Tom and Colleen both laughed, and both tried to be silent as they carried the picture and Pebble back into Jenny's room, but it was too late. Jenny sat up in bed, rubbing her eyes and yawning.

"Jenny, look. Colleen made a painting. Jenny is beautiful."

Jenny pushed up in bed and stared up at the painting. She admired her mother's watercolor paintings and wanted to try painting too. This one was extra special because it was of her and Pebble.

60

"Mommy, can I have it in my room? I really like it."

"Of course, you can have it. Let me frame it and we'll put it on your wall so you and Pebble can see it. Okay?"

"Thank you, Mommy."

"You are absolutely welcome. I had a great time painting it."

"Love you," Jenny said, and gave a big kiss to each her mommy, daddy and Pebble.

A day later, Colleen finally put finishing touches on the watercolor, and she looked for a frame to put it in. She finally found one that matched the wood in Jenny's bedroom. She thought it looked wonderful, but she thought it would look even better if it had a mat to frame the painting under the glass. So, she rolled the painting up and put it and the wood frame in the closet until she would have time to get to the store to get a mat.

Chapter 8

Drones had changed a lot in the thousands of years since the people of Maven had escaped their expanding star. Modern drones being sent out could navigate with great efficiency and had more capabilities. The People of Maven had continued to improve their drones as they learned about each area of space as they travelled through. They had looked at potential homes, but they wanted something similar to the home they had lost. Maven had been a beautiful world and would be hard to replace. The area of space with the most potential world surprised them when they ran across a species that was not friendly. They continued looking and found some planets that were being interfered with by this neighboring planet that seemed to thrive on stealing from other planets rather than working on their own world. But, by this time, they decided that there seemed to be dangerous neighbors throughout the universe, and they determined that maybe they could do something about it. They set out to bring peace to their new area of space. It took a thousand years to gain trust, but they finally negotiated a working relationship with the neighboring worlds.

They programmed this particular drone to patrol a region of space far from the new home world. Suddenly it picked up a strange, and very old signal. The drone automatically marked the area that the signal had come from and sent an acknowledgement. Then it sent a message back to the new home world, giving its coordinates. It didn't assign any significance to the signal. One of its duties was to respond to reports from old drones sent out centuries before and still wandering in space or on the surface of worlds, and carrying out their programming of seeking new worlds.

The drone noted the area of space where the signal had originated, and it turned in that direction. It reported the shift in its direction and proceeded to fly through the darkness of space while it waited for the old signal to repeat.

Its report arrived at the Astro Communication Center that coordinated all the reports of drones patrolling their assigned areas of space. After it entered a queue, the message received an analysis and a priority code. The code came up on the technician's screen and she noted the shift of direction of the receiving drone, but the original sent signal was somewhat different. One, it came from an extremely old drone, and most of those had been accounted for in the intervening years; and two, it didn't seem to come from a source that was freely moving which meant it was probably on an orbiting world. She marked it for further investigation and sent it on down the line.

The next stop was cataloguing. At that station, the drone number was automatically checked and the time of the report registered. The people kept complete histories of all drones sent out from the first group to the last group before the sun expanded. A few were still out there. The people wanted to account for all of them. So many had ceased to exist because of the many dangers in space, but there was still a small number that they were seeking. Finding the old code took a little longer, but eventually the information went on to the next step. They decided to flag it when it reached evaluation.

"Now this is fascinating. It's ancient. Look here," Zebut said to his co-worker. "It was one of the last ones fired before the home world exploded. It had sent out routine reports from five different parsecs before it went silent. Curious, it is suddenly reporting again. I wonder what happened to it in the time between. Display star map please."

A large star map immediately floated in the air all around him. He quickly ordered the parsec he was interested in to enlarge. It was the last parsec that the old drone had travelled through before it went silent.

"Let's see what is in this parsec," he said as he strolled around inside the map. "Highlight the drones in that area."

Red dots appeared through the map, but one was blue at the edge of the parsec.

"Produce a directional cone from the receiving drone toward the sending drone."

A cone shape appeared with the small end starting at the receiving drone and then flaring out in one direction. Several dots appeared in various parts of the cone, with one blue dot on its edge.

"Enlarge cone area," he ordered and the cone shape gambit of stars, asteroids and space debris surrounded him. "Flag and prioritize as number 1."

He turned and looked to his coworker.

"I think I'll wait and see if another report comes in to narrow the search. Do you have anything interesting coming in right now?" he asked his co-worker.

"Not right now, I have essentially all recent reports and I have nothing that is as remote as yours. Do you want me to monitor the area for you?"

At Zebut's bow, the co-worker asked the room computer to highlight the area and requested an immediate alert if anything changed or if another report was sent.

—∽—

Later, after a long day of exploration, Pebble sent his report for the day and settled down to recharge. It had found that its capabilities expanded as it explored the house and when it used the computer. It became excited when any new ability manifested.

Days later, a strange sensation woke Pebble from resting mode. A tingling deep inside became more persistent. It took a few minutes for it to recognize an incoming signal. It got very agitated, because it hadn't received a message since they tested it long ago on its home planet.

"Message received, sending drone number 900473 to assess your situation. Message over."

Pebble sat in stunned silence, then it twirled in place in the jubilation of finally receiving a response after such a long time. A message was such an unexpected thing, it had given up on ever receiving any kind of response.

Why was the message so short? it wondered. Space travel and messages could take centuries as they travelled through vast distances of space. It considered other possible reasons. *Could it be that, to my makers, it had not been gone what seemed a long time?* Pebble's thoughts filled with questions. The message did not say when the drone would arrive. Pebble trembled in reaction as it turned to rush to speak to Tom. It rolled off of the desk and out the door. There it hesitated because it didn't know where Tom's bedroom was located. It turned down the hallway to the first room it saw, this it scanned and dismissed as it did not have a bed in it. It only contained porcelain and other things it didn't recognize. It continued down the hallway to the next room and peeked inside. There was a bed, so it entered. Pebble saw a hand dangling down off the side of the bed, so it jumped up onto the hand. Colleen yelped and jerked her hand up, causing Pebble to land on the bed by her head. It quickly rolled away toward Tom, who woke with a start. Pebble rolled away from the startled people and waited.

"What...?" Tom rubbed his eyes as he tried to wake up. "Colleen, are you ok? What's wrong?"

Colleen looked around, but it was too dark, so she turned on her small lamp on the table beside of bed. Looking around, she spied Pebble.

"That's what's wrong," she said, pointing to Pebble. Tom turned around in surprise.

"Pebble, what's wrong?" Tom asked.

"My people are coming." Pebble replied.

"What do you mean, your people are coming?"

"My people are coming to find me."

"How? Why? When?" Tom asked, bewildered, trying to shake the cobwebs out of his brain.

"I sent reports. Now they come." Pebble spun in a circle.

"What reports? You were in a geode for thousands of years, when did you send reports?"

"I always sent reports, not sure they were successful, no contact. Till now."

Tom's mind was racing. *This would be a first contact scenario. What were the protocols? I don't know; I'm a finance person, not military, but I work for a corporation that has military contacts. I need to tell someone, but who? If I tell the wrong person, the military could get involved, and I don't want that. I can't see what strategic importance the military could find in a little pebble, but they could take Pebble apart to see what made it work. But was it his duty to report the little pebble? What were the repercussions if he reported it, or what were the repercussions if he didn't? Frankly, he didn't know what he should do. He wasn't thinking logically or clearly. I need coffee.*

"Tom, what are we going to do?" Colleen asked.

"Get some coffee and after that, I don't know," Tom said. He pulled his hair back from his face as he shifted up off the bed.

"It will break Jenny's heart if Pebble is taken away." Suddenly, she had another terrifying thought. "Tom, what if Pebble's people are dangerous to us? I mean, to Earth?"

"I know, but I know we will have to do something and soon." Tom turned to the little pebble. "Let's discuss this in the kitchen while we get some coffee and wake up a little more."

Colleen picked up Pebble and carried the agitated pebble out of the room. She stopped at Jenny's room and peeked in to see if she was still asleep. Satisfied Jenny was undisturbed, she went back into the hall.

Everyone moved down the hall to the kitchen and Colleen made coffee for Tom and herself while Tom continued to ask questions of Pebble after placing it on the kitchen island. The soft light from the under-cabinet lighting helped to soothe everyone's nerves. Tom took a deep breath and continued his examination of the small pebble.

"What exactly did the message say? Can you repeat it word for word?"

Pebble repeated the message, word for word, and Tom jumped on one part of it.

"They said they were sending a drone. That's different from sending people. Are they friendly? Are they dangerous? You might reassure them you are fine. Or do you want them to come and get you?"

Pebble was silent for a while as it searched its databanks on Maven history. It didn't find any indication of violence after the People realized their danger from their star. All their people had come together to survive the destruction of their world. And then it thought about the probability of it being picked up and rejoined with the people who had made it. It had been one of millions sent out thousands of years ago. They had produced it for one purpose, so it couldn't answer the questions Tom and Colleen asked it. Would its makers really take it away or would they take its information and discard it or would they just store its information or store Pebble itself? Pebble didn't know. Nothing about what happened after sending reports was in its data banks. Then it thought of Tom, Colleen and Jenny, especially Jenny. Before it was just one of many, now it belonged to a family. "I want to stay with you."

"Okay, when they contact you again, just let them know you are happy here." Colleen said. "Wouldn't that work? Would they leave you here with us?"

"I don't know."

Tom said to Pebble, "I fear if they come, our military here will get involved. Our planet has many countries and they all have their own militaries. Our planet is not a friendly planet, even to our own people. I would tell your people to stay away. Do you know if they are a nonviolent people? There are just too many questions that we don't have answers to right now."

Colleen laid a hand on Tom's arm and said, "Tom, we have to have a strategy. We have no timeline for when they are coming. It could be now or hundreds or thousands of years from now. If they are hostile… we have to prepare. If they are friendly, well, we still have to prepare."

Tom pulled at his hair again and said, "How about I contact our geologist? She has some connections to the military, but I think she would do that for us or, at least, she could be discreet."

"Yes, let's do that. It's a start."

Chapter 9

The room was sparse and filled with forgotten cups of coffee. The semi-circle of stations was set in three tiers, so it was easy to see the timeline displayed from the various stations on the wall at the front of the room. Everyone could see it, including the tiered offices behind the hub. The relaxed and sleepy people manned the room. They were alert to any signal, but it had been a long, boring day again. There were always a lot of signals coming into the hub, but most were from the background noise of the universe or fast radio bursts from known sources like pulsars. They calibrated the machines to send a sound if they found anything that stood out as different. That left the scientists and technicians with almost nothing to do over long spans of time. Deep space transmissions happened all the time, but they were often routine, most reported as background radiation, the normal noise of star lives. Other telescopes covered the visual sky, looking for quasars, gas giants in remote galaxies, and the creation of new stars. Space was a very noisy place, and looking for one signal amongst the cacophony of noise was like looking for a needle in a haystack.

It was Benton Deep Space Sensing Corporation's job, also known as Benton, to look for an answer to the question, "are we alone in the universe?" They worked by listening to the sounds from space.

A simple sound from one keyboard had everyone's head whipping around in surprise. The technician in charge of that station rushed over to check the readout on his screen.

"Signal detected, Sir. Verification initiated." He said in a soft voice.

Officers, including Dr. Alex Meyer, the Signal Processing Manager, strolled over to stand behind him. The technician was so focused and excited he didn't even notice the entourage beginning to encircle his back. Minutes ticked away as they all awaited verification. Finally, another simple sound came from the computer.

"Verification done. Isolating direction," the same soft voice said.

Again, they all waited in silence and again, it was several tense minutes. Another simple sound came from the computer, but this time the printer poked a single sheet of paper into the Output Tray. The technician scanned the sheet and handed it to the Duty Officer, who scanned it and handed it to the Signal Processing Manager.

"What's in this quadrant of space?" He asked as he handed the scan to a technician manning another station. Again, silence ensued as everyone waited for the results.

The Signal Processing Manager had a sudden idea and turned to another technician. "Do we have the capacity to listen for any kind of reply being sent back?"

The technician looked blank for a moment and then responded, "Sir, we only scan for incoming signals, we don't have the ability to look for outgoing ones." She looked uncomfortable for a moment and said, "Sir, the Earth is always sending out noise into space. We are a very noisy planet, sir."

"You are right." He nodded to the woman technician. "Do any of the branches of government have that capability?" he wondered aloud.

"What about ISMC?" she asked.

The manager slowly turned his head and looked at the woman who blushed and ducked. The Manager nodded and turned to his aide. "I need to alert the director, and then, maybe call ISMC and ask them. Keep me informed if anything else develops." he ordered. "Good thinking," he said as he gave the technician a small smile.

Minutes went by as everyone waited to hear if ISMC had that capability. The manager knew they sent and received messages from the various spacecraft on missions into deep space. They had manned and unmanned missions and handled many types of communications. Benton had been going for a long time too, but only had audio telescopes all over the world. They had also established other ways of tracking signals from space - optical, radio, satellite, and laser. They searched 24/7 for any signal from outer space, but did not search for outgoing signals.

When he reached his office, he asked for all information on the signal ASAP and started an inquiry for protocols for incoming signals. He found the protocols right away because Benton had been anticipating a signal from an intelligent source for decades. His assistant soon brought in a file folder with all the information on the received signal. He took a moment to take a few deep breaths to calm his excitement. This primitive planet was driving him crazy. He could finally get his primary job done, and he didn't have a lot of time to do it. First, he needed to send a signal to his true superior that they had identified a signal, and then he headed out to do his other tasks. After picking up a pair of wire cutters that he hid in a pocket, he shoved up from his desk and headed out of his office.

"I'll be back in a few minutes," he told his assistant, as he hurried down the hall to the stairway. He knew where the cameras were so he easily evaded them as he headed down. He went down to the deepest tunnel and the almost forgotten controls by those who worked above, but he had checked this building from top to bottom when he had first come to work there. Now he could use this knowledge to do his real task. He stopped in front of an electrical cabinet. It was a simple matter to open the cabinet and flipped or unplugged several cables and cut a few more. He went down several more cabinets and repeated the process, and when done, erased his fingerprints off the surfaces. He headed back up the stairwell, again avoiding the cameras. When he reached his office, he picked up the file and pretended to read and waited. His assistant came rushing back into the room.

"The director wants to speak to you. He said it was classified."

"Thank you, Mike. I'll be in the director's office if anything else happens." he said as he hurried to the office of Dr. Henry Evans with the file in hand.

Chapter 10

D r. Malinda Gold was already in her office an hour before the start of the workday when Tom arrived.

"Good very early morning, Malinda." he said cheerfully as he stood in the doorway to her office.

"Why, good morning to you too, Tom. Aren't you early for visiting my office? Why didn't you just call?"

"Well, yes, it is early, and I can come back at a more favorable time if you want, but I need to talk privately with you."

"No, that's okay. I like to get here early on most days. It allows me more time to catch up on paperwork. What can I do for you?"

"Well." he hesitated as he pulled his hair. "I have something very important to ask you, but I need your word not to talk about it to anybody, unless I give you permission."

Malinda stared at him as she thought over what he had just said. She hesitated as she thought of her obligations she could not compromise, but again how would she know unless he opened up to her about whatever it was.

"Okay, let's talk about this for a moment. First, you want me to listen to what you have to say, but I have to promise not to tell anyone about it. Question: If after learning what you have to say I am compromised, or the safety of the United States is compromised, will you give me permission to tell someone?"

Tom responded, "I don't think it is something that will compromise you or the United States."

"Okay, then. Second, is it something personal?"

"Well, yes, and no."

"Tom, you are not giving me much to go on here."

"I know, I'm sorry. How about we start over? It relates to the little stone I showed you."

"Oh, okay, but why all the secrecy?"

Instead of responding, Tom took Pebble out of his pocket and put it on her desk, but when he took his hand away, he found Pebble under his fingers again. "Here, now, it's okay. You met her before." Tom moved his fingers away again, this time Pebble stayed. Tom told Pebble, "be polite and say hello to Malinda."

Malinda looked from Tom to the stone and back again.

Pebble turned to her, and in a tiny voice said, "hello, Doctor Malinda."

"What?" she said as she stared at the pebble.

"We had some suspicions off and on for a couple of days. We, or, really Jenny, named it Pebble and later Colleen and Jenny thought they saw it looking at things. I came home the other night, and it had moved. We started watching and talking to it and finally hit on communicating by binary code. That was the breakthrough. Pebble now can translate words from its language into ours."

"Wait, you mean, it can speak, or I mean initiate language? What it just said was not rote? Or a trick? Or a recording of some kind? Or a programmed toy?"

"No, we now speak in English," Tom said. "Jenny named it Pebble, and it answers to that name. Go on, try it."

Malinda took a deep breath and turned to Pebble. "Hello Pebble. Do you know me?"

"Yes, Doctor Malinda."

"Okay, what are you?"

"I am a sensor drone, #3022847, and I was sent from my planet, Maven, to detect other planets that are free of other potential life and might be available to colonization. If I found one, I was to report back."

"You say you were to report back. Who did you report to?"

"I sent reports out into space in the hope they would be picked up by my people. My makers sent millions of us because our sun was going to consume our planet."

"Did they find a new home?"

"I do not know."

"How did you get into a geode? How long have you been on our planet?"

"I became trapped in a gas-filled bubble that became trapped in magma. You said that was about 10 to 12 thousand years ago. I had not been on the planet long before that. I had counted the planetary rotations, days in your language, before I

81

became trapped, there were 3,548 of them which is 9.72 of your years before the volcano exploded."

Tom said, "This next part is the sensitive part, Malinda. I need your promise now."

Malinda thought long and hard about her obligations, *one of them was to search out knowledge of the unknown. Being a geologist gives me a certain amount of wriggle room. We sent a geologist to our nearest planet, the moon, to find the genesis rock to prove that the moon had once been part of the earth. I acknowledge that I really want to know the whole story. This is a first contact protocol. I know that some branches of government had set protocols in place. My field, geology, has nothing like that in place. Maybe it's time for some negotiation.*

"Okay, what we know so far is that this is a first contact situation. If this next part is something that is dangerous to the United States, I might have to report it, but I can say I won't do anything till I talk to you."

Tom looked at her and then looked at Pebble. "Malinda, is there a private room I can use to talk to Pebble?"

"Sure, right there. It's a sealed room for working with harmful materials."

"Come with me, Pebble," Tom said and walked toward the room.

Malinda watched in amazement as Pebble jumped down to a nearby chair and then onto the floor and rolled into the room. Tom closed the door with a last look of amusement at Malinda.

"Anymore messages at all?" Tom asked it.

"No."

"Well, I need to talk to you about this. If Malinda thinks this is important enough to report it to the military, all of our lives will change. They could take you away from Jenny, Colleen, and me. They could do tests on you or they could try to take you apart to see what makes you work."

"Tom, I traveled through space for thousands of your years. We were made to endure a plunge through a planet's atmosphere, and I have already survived thousands of years in a geode. There is a high probability that I would survive any tests."

"Do you want to trust her?"

"Yes, Tom."

"All right, let's do this."

Tom opened the door and Pebble rolled out and across the floor. There it jumped up onto the chair and then up to the desktop.

"Dr. Malinda, Tom is very distressed because I have received a message."

Malinda's eyes narrowed in thought. "A message? What did it say?"

Pebble, again, repeated the message exactly.

"Did you respond?"

There was a brief silence as Pebble searched its memory banks.

"No."

"Okay, so we know that a drone is on its way to find Pebble. What can we do about it?"

"I thought you might know someone, who you trust, to tell this to and get some feedback or opinions of what to do," Tom told her.

"Yes, I do know someone who works in a nearby building. Dr. Daniel Cooper in telecommunications."

"I know of him, but haven't met him. What does he do in telecommunications?"

"He oversees the security protocols and investigates new telecommunicating technologies. I'll keep you informed."

"Okay, he sounds good. Thanks Malinda."

Chapter 11

"Yes, Harold, it's Henry Evans. Don't sputter. I told Alex to call you. We have a situation over here at Benton-Houston that maybe you can help us with."

"I already told that signal processing manager of yours to tell you about the situation and then you can determine if it's classified or not," the director of International Space Mining Corporation, Harold Cummings sputtered. "Is this phone secure, Henry?"

"Yes, Harold, it's secure. It's Benton, for crying out loud."

"Maybe you should fly up here to Atlanta and we'll talk about this. I can't take a chance."

"Harold, it might be too late if I have to fly there." he heard mutterings and said, "okay, okay, I'll come. See you in a few hours. Bye."

"Mary! Get us seats on the next military plane to Atlanta. Duty Officer, get all data on that signal, ASAP. Mary, you're with me. Let's go people."

Mary hurried to keep up with the him. They grabbed their emergency suitcases and the paperwork the director would need when he met with the ISMC director.

Director Henry Evans of Benton-Houston walked into Director Harold Cummings' office at ISMC three hours after talking to him on the phone and saw his friend buried in paperwork. He shuttered.

"Harold, please come up for air," he teased.

Harold's head popped up over the top of the towering stack on his desk. "Oh, Henry, you made good time."

"Yes, we hopped on military transport. I need to talk to you about something extraordinary. I really don't ask lightly."

"We? Who did you bring with you?"

"I brought Mary Matthews, my assistant. Is that a problem?"

"No, no, it's okay. Tell me about what is so important, but I can't promise anything. Just so you know."

"Our Benton-Houston office has intercepted a signal coming from space. That's documented and my people believe it is from an entity and not a natural origin from space, which makes it unique. It could be from an intelligent source and that would take more investigation. But that's not what we want to ask of you. If this is a contact, and someone on Earth sent back a response, could we track it?"

Harold sat looking at his hands for a long time thinking.

"ISMC sends commands and messages all the time, and also you receive answering messages from spacecraft and mines all the time. What's the problem?" Henry questioned him. "Maybe they already sent a response."

Harold looked up at his friend. "The military has a protocol in place that involves us. Yes, we can do what you ask, but you have to go through the military."

"You know if the military gets involved, we could be looking at months of politics. I'm a retired member of the military and it takes a long time to get things done. Good people, but it has a lot of red tape. I just want to catch the response if there is one."

"Okay, Henry, I have a meeting coming up in an hour. I'll bring up the problem in a round-about way and keep your name out of it. I'll call you as soon as I get some feedback."

"I really can't ask for more than that. Here, I have a copy of our data if you want it. Thanks Harold."

The director handed over the printouts and left the office.

Henry walked out of the ISMC headquarters and Mary called a transport to take them to their hotel. There he went to his room and stretched out on the bed. He badly needed sleep; it had been a long day. The hotel operator called promptly at 5pm to wake him for dinner. Henry hated eating alone, so he invited Mary to join him in the hotel dining room. Henry also called the Benton office to see if any more signals had come through. It disappointed him to get an answer in the negative. He took a long, satisfying shower and dressed in clean clothes that felt like heaven after being in the same clothes all day. He felt like a new man.

"Good evening, Mary. I hope you didn't have plans," he said in a cheery voice. He really liked his assistant because she was a serious young woman, but without being pushy or antisocial. He liked someone who had good sense. He felt he could explain something he wanted done, and it would get done. He didn't have to explain things over and over. She also had initiative, that was important, but above all, he trusted her.

"Well, let's eat," as he ushered her to their table. There he saw several young men look toward their table. He didn't for a moment think the looks were for him. He looked at his young assistant who was busy reading the menu. He could see a slight flush creeping up her neck as she ignored their glances. Henry hid his smile. He remembered what his assistant was going through, because thirty-five years ago he had been one of those admirers of a lovely young lady eating in a restaurant. He had tentatively started a conversation and a year later had married to the love of his life. He had shared a long and happy life of years of marriage and four children and seven grandchildren so far. Yes, he had a good life and he wished that for Mary. He also had a handsome young son of the right age. He wouldn't mind if that son met his assistant. He hoped his son wouldn't hesitate to ask Mary out because of him.

"Do you want to stay here to eat? Can we go somewhere else if you want?" he asked.

"No, this is okay. I think I'll have the salad and a steak."

"Oh, that sounds good to me too. Would you order for both of us, Mary? Oh, and I would like a beer. I'll be right back."

"Yes, okay," Mary said as she reached for the order module to enter their order.

Henry returned and they relaxed into easy talk about family and the fast approaching holidays. He took advantage of the time to show her pictures of his children and grandchildren. He put a little extra stress on his middle son and was rewarded with a flicker of her eyelashes. He changed the topic with a slight smile on his face.

"So, what are your holiday plans?" he asked as he put his photos back in his wallet.

"Mom says she wants to have Christmas at the farm. The house is big enough, even for our large family," Mary mused with a small smile on her face.

"I remember the farm. You took me there when you first became my assistant. Beautiful place. I really liked the natural woodwork."

"Yes, that woodwork was my grandfather's pride and joy. He did the same woodwork at my uncle's farm in Kentucky too."

Their orders arrived and for the next few minutes they both delved into their meals.

His cell phone beeped, and he took his leave to take the call out in the hall. He came back to his seat smiling.

"Would you like me to order our transport?" she inquired as he moved to sit.

"No, no, finish your meal," he told her as he also started eating again.

She wondered what the phone call was about, but knew Henry would tell her if she needed to know. She was very grateful to be the assistant to this director. Some directors were disgraces to their positions, but not this one, who she always thought of as her director.

"Dessert?" Henry asked.

"No, thank you."

"Well, me neither."

They left the hotel and walked down the main street, just window shopping. Soon they came to the subway entrance and the director signaled to go down. They got tickets and boarded the train. A few stops later, they got off the car and went back to the surface. There they got a taxicab and traveled to the Atlanta museum where they spent about an hour strolling around.

Mary automatically checked how long they had travelled around the city. If they were being pursued, she might need to leave without her and the Director's things, which were just clothes anyway. She had all the important papers in her large handbag.

"I think that should do it," Henry said.

"Do you have anything important in your hotel room?" Mary asked as she checked to see if they had been followed. "May I make a suggestion? If we take a taxi back to our hotel, we could ask it to go pass by several blocks, and then we could double back on foot."

"Yes, I think we will do that. Keep your eyes out."

"Yes, will do."

After following the suggestion, they were approaching the hotel from a side street when Mary recognized a man dressed in black loitering against the wall.

"I think that is one of the men from the restaurant." she informed the director, and they went into a coffeehouse on the side street that let them see the hotel entry without being seen.

"Can you tell me why are we being followed?" she asked quietly.

"I wish I knew, but I got a call from a friend to be extra careful. There seems to be cause for vigilance."

"How about I go in the back way and see about bringing your clothes? Then we can get you another hotel room."

The director thought about it for a while. "You sure? They could check out my hotel room or have the back watched."

"I'll be careful."

"Okay, try it, but I don't want anything to happen to you. If you get caught, just give up. I'll watch from here and I'll try to find out why we need these maneuvers." he moved into the bathroom where he locked the door after everyone was out. Then he called Harold. "What's going on? I've been running around like I'm enemy number one."

Harold said. "Keep running. Don't know exactly what's up, but they have your Benton Houston office on ice too."

"What? Benton-Houston? They're mostly just young kids and scientists. What the heck is going on?"

"Don't know. Maybe you should just give up and see what they want. Got to go. Good luck."

Mary left and began her flanking movement to get to the back entrance to the hotel. She moved easily and took advantage of cover along the way. It didn't take her long to gain access through the staff entrance. She moved up the back stairs to the director's floor. There she looked out and saw two men also dressed in black move out of the room and come in her direction. She quickly moved up the stairway until no one could see her from the stairway door of the director's floor. There she waited until she heard the door open and close, and then she moved back down and opened the door to check. No one was on the floor or near the director's door. She had the room key so entry was quick. She was through the door in seconds and quietly checking the rooms. She noted the clothes messily thrown on the bed and the director's suitcase slashed on the inside. She wondered why all the secrecy. She quickly gathered his things into the suitcase and took it out to the trash chute. She quickly sent the suitcase down the chute to the trash bin outside. She re-locked the door and moved to the stairs and down to the trash bin. There she retrieved the suitcase and was away before anyone noticed.

It surprised the director to see his assistant walk down the side street away from the hotel carrying his suitcase. Going out the back door of the coffee shop, he hurried to catch up with her. Together, they walked to a less affluent hotel and reserved two rooms.

In one of the new rooms of the new hotel, they both looked at each other.

"Well, the way I see it, I have two options. Keep running not knowing why, or turning myself in and finding out why. Harold told me that they have rounded up the kids at Benton-Houston. We have to know why all this is happening. Can you go to your uncle's farm, it's closer, and stay for a while? You have my papers; they may be what they want. Harold also has a copy, but I don't know if he turned them over to these people. You can study them and see if you can find anything important in them. Be safe and keep those papers safe. They could be our only copy. Oh, I think it might be unwise to use your credit cards. Do you need any cash?"

"No need, I have money and I promise not to use my credit cards. Are you sure you don't want me to come with you? You might need me, and two people might find out more than just one person.

"No, I think one of us should stay free to move, just in case."

"I'll call my uncle to let him know I'm coming and warn him to be careful and don't tell anyone that I'm coming or that I called."

"Mary, I need you free. Don't get caught. Do you understand?" he said in his most commanding voice.

"Yes, Henry." She eyed him warily, trying to read his anxiety.

"Promise me you'll go to your uncle's and stay safe. I need you to study those papers, they might give us the answer we need. Please."

"I promise to do my best." She reassured him.

"Okay, get going. I think they will find me soon. Try to find out anything you can." he gave her a hug. "Be safe."

"I will, and you stay safe too," she said as she left.

The director sighed and closed the door. He went to the bed and stretched, wondering how long it would take. Two hours later, a knock on the door woke him.

Chapter 12

D r. Malinda was very busy, but she wanted to start on what she promised Tom and Pebble. She had to admit to herself; she was hooked on Pebble. Too bad Jenny and Pebble were a solid team. They should be together; they were good for one another. If Jenny had Pebble taken away from her, she would be devastated, and who knew what would happen to Pebble or the anguish that would cause Jenny, she thought.

"Is Dan free to talk, this is Malinda Gold?" she asked his administrative assistant.

"Malinda." Dan's voice came over the line. Crisp and English, but with an undertone of laughter. She could listen to him speak all day and he and his wife had been friends of hers for years. "What can I do for you today? I know, go to Paris with me and the wife, or down to Hawaii where we all can swim in the surf." Dan was in his late-70s and he loved to tease the girls as he called them. His wife usually just shook her head.

"Dan, I'm calling to ask you some questions. Do you have a few minutes now? I'll come to your office if it's okay."

"Sure, come on down."

Dr. Malinda hurried down the stairs to the tunnel that ran underground to the other buildings. Negotiating that labyrinth was always a tasking job. It had lots of people moving through the many branching tunnels going in different directions to different buildings. Co-workers told stories of a man who came into the tunnels at night when no one was around because he wanted to count how many tunnels really existed. He was never seen again. Some personnel refused to use the tunnels because of that story. Malinda had travelled this labyrinth many times, so she made good time walking the distance to Dan's office. She made the trip in ten minutes flat. *That must be my personal best*, she thought. Dan's office was on the 10th floor of the Telecommunications Building. Malinda had always appreciated the beautiful artwork on the walls on his floor. Finally, she approached his office door. She could hear him arguing with someone, even though she couldn't hear the other end of the conversation. He saw her approach the door, but could see her quickly turn around and retreat. Overhearing other people's conversations was not something she wanted to do, so she moved off down the hall.

"Sorry about that," he said, waving her toward his office. He seemed distracted, and a little disturbed.

"Anything wrong?" she asked.

"Yes, but it's not something you can do anything about. What can I do for you?"

"Do you have an area that is a quiet room? I want to ask you something sensitive."

He looked surprised by the request, but not upset. "Right this way." he moved down the hallway to a glass-enclosed room with double doors. He moved through them and down a short hall to another set of doors. He gestured her inside and moved behind her to lock the doors and flipped a switch that turned on the baffles that completely surrounded them. "Okay, the room is activated and you can say whatever you want."

"I need an opinion from you. It's important."

Okay," he said hesitantly. "Will I be in trouble if I hear this?"

"I don't know," she answered honestly.

"Life is interesting, isn't it? I have built a career over five decades and now might throw it all away. Tell me."

"Okay, I have met an entity from outer space and it wants to stay and play with Jenny."

"What? Are you kidding me? Who's Jenny?"

"Sadly, no, I'm not kidding you. I'm not explaining this very well."

"Start at the beginning, please."

"Okay." and she did, sharing Pebble's story which included where Jenny came into the story. "Well, what do you think, do you know of anyone we can contact?"

"We?" he demanded.

"Oh, dear. I meant me...ur, I, I meant for me to contact."

"We can just say you and another person want to know if I know of someone you can talk to about our visitor. Yes?"

"Perfect."

"Malinda, I'm sorry I can't help you, but not because I don't want to, but because I just spoke with someone I trust. He told me they have rounded up the Benton - Houston people and no one can talk with them. Right now, he is tied up trying to help with that situation. Sorry."

"Benton's? What's going on? Sounds like the military has gotten into it," she murmured.

"What you want to ask me is connected with the military?" he asked sharply.

Malinda paced away from him and thought for a minute, nodded and turned back to him with her mind made up on what to tell him.

"We need to get some guidance on informing the military about our visitor. Pebble is a drone of sorts that landed on our planet thousands of years ago and became entombed in a geode as it formed. My friend purchased the geode to bring home to his daughter and when they broke it open the drone fell out. Since then, the drone has learned a lot about our planet and also learned our language. Its mission was to find other suitable planets to colonize and report back to its people, which it did, but now it has received a message from them. The message was that another drone is coming to check on it."

"Oh no, first contact. There are protocols in place, but no one ever wanted to enact them. Well, that explains the news I got right before you arrived. Benton personnel in Houston are on lockdown and they escorted Dr. Henry Evans to Quantico for debriefing."

"Why Benton in Houston?"

"Allegedly, they picked up the incoming message."

"Why don't we get in touch with whoever you would suggest and find out what to do?" she asked him.

"Director Evans at Benton was the person I would recommend," he said.

"Can we contact someone else and ask who he would recommend?"

"Director Evans was the last person who Director Harold Cummings at ISMC met with before all this happened," he said thoughtfully.

"Oh dear. Now what do we do? Do you know anyone else?" she asked as she wondered how to tell Tom. "Should we give Pebble up to the authorities?"

"Pebble?" he asked with his eyebrows lifted in astonishment.

"It is the size of a small pebble, hence the name. The daughter named it; so the only person you know that could help us was this director of Benton - Houston?"

"There is one other person I can think of to call. Give me a minute." he turned from her to go back to his office. He quickly dialed the number for Harold Cummings at ISMC. "Harold, hello, I'm calling because I just got some distressing news about Henry at Benton's. Do you know anything about it?"

He listened for a while. "That is a mystery, all right. I wonder what the military would want with him. Maybe I'll find out what all this about some day. Sorry, to disturb you. Goodbye." he stood in silence, thinking about what had not been said in the brief conversation.

"Well?" asked Malinda when he returned to the quiet room.

"That is an interesting question. I spoke to Harold Cummings at ISMC. He told me that Henry had come to him yesterday asking if ISMC could track a message that Benton had intercepted and also see if ISMC could track any answering message from Earth. Harold told Henry that he would have to go through the military. What was not said was if Harold had called the military and put them onto Henry and Benton."

"Why would he do that?" Malinda demanded.

"Protocol, my dear. ISMC and the military are partners in a lot of political operations. They could consider Pebble a threat."

"Yes, I can see that, matter of fact, I had suggested it myself."

"To whom did you suggest it? Come clean, Malinda. We might want to warn this person."

"I know you're right, but it isn't just one person, it's a family."

"Who? Do I know him or them?"

"Yes, it's Tom Baumgardner and his family. Let's go get him and fill him in, okay?"

"Okay, let me close up some things and I'll meet you at Tom's office in a few minutes.'

Chapter 13

Tom was pacing his office as he waited to hear from Malinda. *I'm really not suited for intrigue,* he thought. He was so excited, but also scared, not so much for himself, but for his family. He didn't want Jenny or Colleen to get hurt.

"Tom, are you okay?" Malinda asked.

He jumped when he heard Malinda's voice from his office door. "Sorry, I'm nervous."

She smiled and came into the small space. "I have someone coming to talk to us. There have been some issues you need to know about."

"What issues?" he asked nervously.

"Well, Tom, we'll get to that in a few minutes." Dan walked into the office and patted Tom's arm. "I think we need to go. I talked to your supervisor about you coming with us for a special project. I didn't tell him what the project was or where we were going, just that I needed you. He was very accommodating."

"What? But where?" he sputtered to a stop when Dan put his finger up to silence him.

"I have a special project that I think you will be the perfect person to help me with. Malinda's coming, too. It will mean a great deal if you two can help. Let's hurry and get there so I can explain more thoroughly," he said as he grabbed Tom's coat for him, and ushered them out the door on the way to get Malinda's coat in her office.

"Of course, Doctor, we would be happy to help in any way we can," Tom said, looking puzzled.

They hurried out the door of the main building and got into Tom's car, as it was the closest. As they turned onto Fifth Avenue, they saw several black SUVs pull into the parking lot behind them.

Dan said in a calm voice, "I think we need to call your family, Tom. I think those men will visit your family soon. Is our visitor with your daughter?"

"Malinda, can you call while I drive? And yes, she has Pebble with her all the time. They are almost inseparable," Tom responded.

"Tom, can you drive past your house with no one observing us?" Dan asked.

"Yes, but why?"

"Let me say this gently. If the military responded so quickly trying to pick us up, they probably already have your family, and if everything looks quiet, it might be a trap for us."

"But my family!" Tom exclaimed.

"Tom, the military won't do anything to your wife or child. They want us, not them. As long as Jenny hides Pebble, they should be okay."

A half-hour later, they coasted two blocks away from Tom's house. Tom circled around the block and parked in a cul-de-sac in a friend's driveway. The backyards backed up to each other behind the houses.

"This is Nate's house, and he is away with his family for a few days and the neighbors all work, so we can park here and go to the back to see what might be going on at my house. Agreed?" Tom informed them anxiously.

They all got out of the car and walked up and along the side of the garage where they gathered behind a large bush. Cautiously, they peered at the back of Tom's house and saw two men in black uniforms standing guard.

Tom's heart broke when he realized that the military was already there and had his family. Colleen who was pregnant and his little Jenny were so defenseless. He wondered if he should just give himself up. Hopefully, Dan and Malinda might not be included in this mess.

They waited a little longer to see what was happening. All seemed quiet. It really was too quiet. Not even a dog barked.

Wait. Tom thought, *no dog barked*. But he knew the Adam's dog down the way on his block was outside all the time. *Where was that dog*? He hoped that they didn't hurt that little dog. It barked at everything. He got a strange feeling of being exposed. "Let's get out of here. Something is not right."

Malinda and Dan looked at him and started to move back to the car. They froze when the military moved to the house next to Tom's and broke down the door. A scream sounded and the military men, also dressed in the same black uniform, came out of the house holding an elderly woman by the arms.

"Oh, crap. I forgot that Maureen's mother was visiting. That's Annette. She's here to watch the house for Maureen and Michael Ross, while they are on a cruise," Tom whispered and grimaced in response to the woman's tirade toward the two men.

They marched Annette over to Tom's back door and waited. Soon they were joined by their superior, who interrogated her. They wanted to know who she was, did she see anything, what was she doing in the house next door.

Tom had to admit the woman had spunk. She interrogated her captors as strongly as they tried to interrogate her. They let her go back to her house with warnings. She turned around and yelled back at them, "You should come in and fix the kitchen you messed up and the table you broke in two," as she shook her fist at them, "and the back door you broke down."

The military men regrouped, and the superior contacted someone on his phone and then gave them orders. Soon all of them moved out of the house and back to their cars.

Tom, Malinda, and Dan looked at each other, unsure if they could trust that they had actually moved out from Tom's house and from his neighbor's house. Tom kept scanning the streets to see if there were any black SUVs moving around the block. Soon, they all relaxed.

"I want to go inside and see if they took anything or maybe left a clue to where they took Colleen and Jenny," Tom said.

"Okay, it looks deserted." Dan tried to sound convinced.

"Do you think it could be a trap?" Tom snapped.

"I don't know, but it seems too easy."

Tom thought a while and said, "all right, let's wait awhile."

"How long do you think we should wait?" Malinda asked.

"Let's wait till dusk, and then gradually approach the house," Dan suggested.

"Sounds okay to me. I just know sitting in the dirt is not doing my clothes any good," Malinda added as she looked down at her brand-new dress.

They waited in silence, not talking because they didn't want to make any noise. Finally, at nearly dusk, they moved back to the car. As quietly as possible, they drove the car around the block and parked down the block from Tom's house. As they started out of the car, Annette, came out of the door of Maureen's house with a trowel in her hand. She moved over to the flowers at the corner of the yard. She got down to her knees and worked the soil. When Tom and his group got close, she whispered, "go around this house and in the back. Tom, don't go into your house. Go down to the basement of my house."

Tom stopped in his tracks and would have spoken, but Dan stopped him, beckoning him to accompany him. Dan led the way as they all moved around the house. Stepping over the debris, they moved in the back door and descended into the basement. As soon as Tom came down the stairs, he was grabbed by a terrified Colleen and Jenny, and he wrapped his arms around them with joy and relief.

Tom could sense the moment Colleen saw Malinda and Dan when she stiffened in his arms.

"Let me introduce everyone. This is Dr. Dan Cooper and Dr. Malinda Gold. This is my wife, Colleen, and my daughter, Jenny. Colleen, they are here to help us find a way out of this mess. Jenny, can you hold up Pebble, so it can see them too."

"Hello Pebble," said Malinda, greeting the small stone. "This is Dr. Dan," she turned to point to Dan.

"Hello, are you here to help us?" Pebble asked.

Looking stunned, Dan responded, "Hello Pebble, I am very glad to meet you and I hope we get to have a long conversation some time. I have about a thousand questions to ask you." Dan bent down to look more closely at the little pebble. "But, first, I think we need to talk strategy," he said to the group.

"Okay, but I don't understand what to do. This is turning my world upside down. I'm not sure how to get my bearings," Tom admitted as he gripped his family tight.

"Before you all get started, why don't you sit down and I'll get something to eat for everyone?" Annette said from the doorway.

"Let me help you with that," Colleen volunteered.

"Better not, dear, we don't want anyone to know you and your family are here."

"You're right."

"Why don't you start by informing us about Pebble?" Dr. Dan asked Colleen.

"I can talk to you, Dr. Dan," Pebble rolled to Dr. Dan.

"I'm sorry Pebble, I should have realized that you could speak for yourself."

"I am a drone and I landed on this planet a long time ago. A volcano erupted and I was trapped when the lava flowed. I rolled into gas and magma. I stayed in the geode that formed for a long time until Tom broke my shell. Jenny picked me up and now I stay with Jenny."

"Tell me about the signal you received, Pebble."

"I received a message from a drone of my people. They had one my reports and were coming."

"So, you sent a report."

"I have sent many reports since I landed on the planet, thousands of your years ago, but never got a message back, until now."

"Do you know when the drone will get here?" Dan asked.

"No."

"No? No idea at all?"

"No."

"Why not?"

"Why not what?"

Dan looked helplessly to Malinda and Tom.

"Let me try," Tom said. "Pebble, can you tell us why you don't know when the drone will get here?"

"I don't know which report the drone is coming about. I sent many reports since I landed."

"I know the military has procedures, but why the heavy hand? That something I don't understand," Malinda commented. "What are the procedures, anyway? Do you know, Dan?"

"I only know a few of the procedures that the military normally follow. One, they secure the perpetrator, two, investigate the scene, and three, interrogate the perpetrator. I'm not sure of the rest of them, and those don't seem to relate to a first contact scenario."

"How do we apply those procedures here?"

"Well, the first one is to secure the perpetrator. I say they are still working on that one. They have the Benton Deep Space Sensing Corporation people from the Houston office, but they don't have us or Pebble. And I think they are still looking for some other people," Dan said, thinking of all the people that they might look for. "One other thing they do that's very upsetting is to take any devices they find apart to investigate what makes them work." he spared a look at Jenny who was holding Pebble tightly.

"You mean they want to open Pebble to see how it works? Daddy, Mommy, we can't let them kill Pebble. Please stop them!" she wept and turned into her mother's arms to be held.

"Jenny, you know we'll do everything we can to not let that happen," Dan told her gently.

"You promise?" Jenny asked him with tears rolling down her cheeks.

"Oh, honey, you can't ask him that. He can only do so much," Colleen said as Dan knelt next to her daughter.

"Jenny, I promise to do everything I can to let nothing happen to Pebble. Okay?" Dan promised.

"I trust Dan, because Tom and Malinda trust Dan, and Dan promised to do his best. Okay?" Pebble added.

"I don't want anything to happen to you. I love you," Jenny told Pebble.

"I love you too."

"I hate to interrupt, but those men are back and they are in your house and some houses down the street," Annette announced from the doorway. "They seem to have some strange-looking equipment that they are pointing at the houses."

"Everyone, be silent in case this equipment is what I think it is," Dan whispered as he hurried up the stairs. Tom followed him as close as possible. Together, they peeked out of the downstairs windows. Dan pantomimed to Annette for a pencil and paper. He scrawled "can you run your sweeper?" She nodded and went to a closet to bring out her vacuum. Tom and Dan went back to the basement to let the rest know what was going on upstairs. The noise of the sweeper started.

Tom gestured for everyone to gather around and he wrote, "we need to be extra quiet and look for a hiding place quick." He hoped the "men in black," for want of a better description of the men, didn't have heat sensing equipment that would pinpoint their heat signatures.

They split up into smaller groups and opened and closed doors and storerooms, seeking. One looked encouraging. It was a very large closet with a false sliding door that opened for additional dress and coat storage, and it had the added benefit of being backed by a standup freezer that would help to hide their heat signatures. It was cold in the area, but they all climbed behind the hanging clothes and were surprised that they all fit inside the space. It was so dark Pebble automatically opened an appendage and made a light so everyone could see. Tom looked around the basement for something to jam the front storage unit shut. He found it in a basket under the stairs. It was a simple piece of wood that they could lay in the track of the front cupboard. He and Colleen had a similar piece of wood that they used to jam the sliding glass door to their patio. He told Pebble to put out the light, and it was a good thing too, because as they were trying it out when the men came to the house demanding to search again. Annette protested, but they forced her out of the way. They made her sit in her living room under guard as they looked everywhere. After going through the main floor and the bedrooms upstairs, they moved into the basement.

"You better not be leaving dirt around my house. I have been cleaning up after you all day. I should make you all stay to dust and sweep, the way you are leaving tracks everywhere."

"Oh, shut up, will you," one man grumbled.

"No, I won't shut up. You should have more respect for your elders and respect for other people's property."

Soon, she heard footsteps coming up the stairs, and she held her breath as she wondered if they had found her new friends. She watched as only the men who had trooped downstairs came back up.

"Where did they go, old lady?" their leader demanded.

"Where did who go? What are you talking about?"

"You know who I'm talking about, the people who live next door. I'm sure you know where everyone is all around this neighborhood."

"I have more important things to do besides spying on my neighbors. Besides, you still haven't fixed what you broke the last time you came calling. Are you going to fix what you and your men did to my daughter's house? I should sue the government for the money."

He threw his hands up into the air and turned to his men. "We're out of here. She knows nothing. Crazy old lady." with that parting shot, the men marched out of the house.

She rushed to the window to watch them go. All the cars headed off, but she still watched the front and back to make sure they didn't come back. When Tom and Dan came up the steps, she put her finger up for them to wait. She got her trowel out and again went out to do some more weeding near the sidewalk. It was getting really dark, but she could see farther down the street that way. She headed around the back to put her trowel away and throw away the weeds she had pulled and saw the back of a black SUV on the street behind. When she went back into the house, she wrote a note telling Dan and Tom what she had seen. They again went downstairs and hid. It was a good thing they did because a few minutes later the men were back.

"Didn't you make enough of a mess the last time you were here?" she yelled at them as she bent to pick up what was left of her back door.

They ignored her and searched both her neighbor's and her house again. She stood there with her arms crossed, shaking her head. Again, they found nothing. She watched them leave for the second time and wondered if they would again return. Surely, everyone was safe, she hoped.

Chapter 14

Mary watched from the woods as her uncle, aunt, and cousin were questioned by strange men, all dressed in black, and driving an SUV. *What information did those men want?* she wondered. Probably, they wanted to know where she was and if they had heard from her. she didn't know why she was on the run, just that Henry told her to run and that it was important. It was a puzzle, and those her only pieces.

Soon, the men seemed satisfied and drove away, but Mary didn't move. She saw in Atlanta how they staked out their hotel, so she waited and scanned the surrounding area for watchers. A few minutes later, she spotted one in the grove of trees to the left of the house. It was a good spot to see most of the entrances to the house. She and her family knew of a secret entrance where she and her cousin used to play the game of hide and seek when they were little. She carefully moved from tree to tree, scanning in case the men had stationed more than one lookout. It only took her a few minutes to gain the side of the house that the watcher could not see. The plants there were thick and provided good cover for her to move along the side of the house as she crawled through the bushes. She spied the entrance to the old coal chute and prayed that they haven't sealed it up since she had last visited. She gently pressed on the panel and it slid open silently, then she moved the catch to release the inner door. Quickly, but also quietly, she sat down and moved off the ledge. The abrupt slide took her breath away, but she didn't have time to steady it because her uncle lifted her up into a huge hug.

"We've been so worried," he said as he gently held her. The rest of the family gathered around her in another hug.

"Let's go upstairs," said her aunt, "and get out of this old coal chute."

"I always liked this old coal chute," Mary said with a smile. "Especially after you cleaned it up and put in a slide so we could play."

"Yeah, we always had a good time sliding down that chute," Davy, her cousin added.

As her family turned to go into the regular basement, she caught her cousin's hand. He gave her a puzzled look.

She wrote a note and handed it to Davy. "I think I need to stay out of sight. There's a man watching the house. I'm sure he's watching to see if I come here. I have so much to tell you, but I think I need to stay in the basement. I also need to hear what they told you."

The men seemed stunned, but her aunt, after a minute, said quietly, "all right then, we'll just make the best of it. Let's get started, we'll make a game of it for the kids, but this is dangerous business. I don't like strange men coming onto our land, questioning and watching us."

They moved out the coal room and shut the door firmly and locked it. Nick, her uncle, got some large towels out and covered the basement windows in the recreation room, and Davy went upstairs for blankets and pillows. Amy, her aunt, called down for Nick to come and get lunch. Nick hurried upstairs, wondering if his wife had lost her mind.

"Did you say lunch?" he asked with a lifted eyebrow, because they had lunched an hour ago. But he didn't need to worry when he saw the basket filled with food.

Amy held up a sign that said, "put this in the refrigerator downstairs."

"Oh," he mouthed.

She set the table for lunch and then went downstairs to find Mary hungerly eating a sandwich from the basket.

Amy wrote on a piece of paper, "those men came into the house and with all the worry and questioning, well, it got me wondering if they might have bugged the place," and looked worried as she looked over at the lampshades.

"Good idea," Nick wrote.

They spread out to cover each room, looking under furniture, around windows, and behind drapes and under rugs. Nick found one in the living room, and Davy found one in the kitchen. Amy had gone upstairs to look in the bedrooms and bathroom. She found one in the bathroom and one in each of the bedrooms, even the children's rooms.

Perverts, the lot of you, she silently thought to herself in outrage.

Mary looked all around the basement and laundry room. She found one in the recreation room and one in the refrigerator. That one made her scratch her head in puzzlement. They all regrouped in the rec room to look at their finds and to determine what to do. Nick made his mind up and got a hammer from the garage. He wanted, more than anything, to take out his fury at this invasion of his home, this threat to his family, on something. He couldn't get to the men, but he could destroy these little spies. He took heavy towels and a flat board and laid the items to muffle the sound.

Mary quickly wrote a note that made him stop and think. He sighed and nodded.

"Thanks for lunch, Amy, but we need to get back to work. Come on Davy, we need to get done with the work in the barn," he grabbed the towel full of bugs and walked up the steps.

"Okay Dad, Excellent lunch mom." he winked at Mary as he walked up the stairs.

Nick and Davy headed out to the barn. Davy wondered what his dad had in mind to do with the bugs.

"We need to move some hay to the fields where the wild horses can get to it. Let's load up the flatbed truck with about nine bales and get moving. It's almost time for the kids to get home from school."

Davy agreed and got the hay loaded quickly and his dad took the towel with its burden of bugs. They headed out to the outlying pastures that the wild horses favored.

"Let's do the farthest first and work our way down."

When they got to the meadow, Davy watched his dad take one bug and unload one bale of hay and dug a small hole with the toe of his boot, drop the bug in and place the bale on top.

He winked at Davy as he got back in the truck. They followed that pattern for about half of the bugs, but the rest got pitched into the pond or forest. They were all smiles when they got back to the barn. Nick started to say something to Davy, but Davy stopped him.

"I want to go down to the house and check on the kids. They should get home soon." Davy informed him.

Amy was dealing with her two grandchildren who were dancing around her and talking to her at the same time.

"Wait, I can't understand both of you at the same time. One at a time, please."

"Grandma, I'm older so I should go first," Mara said in a very matter-of-factly voice, looking up through her eyelashes.

"Okay, Mara, you will go first."

"It's not fair, Grandma, just because she's older, she always gets her way."

"I promise that next time you can go first, Jimmy. All right?"

"All right," he said reluctantly.

"Hey guys, we have a surprise for you," Davy grabbed Mara and whirled her around till she giggled.

"My turn," yelled Jimmy, as he jumped up and down in his excitement.

Davy grabbed Jimmy and lifted him over his head and then dropped him down into his arms to tickle him until he was helpless with laughter.

Nick and Amy stood back, smiling as Davy played with his kids.

"Wish Christine was home to enjoy this. She'll be home from the office soon."

"Why don't you kids go down to the rec room and see your surprise," Nick told his excited grandkids.

"What is it, Grandpa?" they asked.

"You'll see."

Mary could hear everything as she listened at the base of the stairs. She quickly looked for a good hiding place. The kids raced down the stairs with Mara in the lead, not sure what or who they would see. There was a lot of pushing and shoving as they moved down the last steps. Mary timed her appearance as the kids stormed past the laundry room door.

"Boo!" she said at their backs. She was rewarded with squeals and jumps of happiness that made her step back quickly to keep her toes from getting trampled.

"Aunt Mary!" they yelled.

"I take you are happy to see me," she laughed as she heard the rest of the family move down the stairs to join them. She smiled at Davy. "They have grown so much since I last saw them."

"Well, they should have grown. They eat everything that isn't moving," he teased.

"Daddy!" they both protested. He shrugged. "Just telling the truth."

"We need a family meeting, but I think we need Christine here for that, so for right now let's play a game. We will pretend to camp, right here in the rec room. Mary will stay down here while she's here. Let's make this cozy for Mary. Let's go, people."

The kids jumped up and started right in moving pillows and blankets to more comfortable places. They kept looking at their grandpa because when he used that voice; they knew he meant business. Working together, they had the room looking good in no time. And Christine walked in.

"Just like you to get home after all the work is done," Davy teased as he gave her a kiss.

"I always had great timing," she shot back at him as she hugged him back.

"Hi Mommy," Mara and Jimmy chimed together as they rushed to give her their hugs too.

"Welcome home. How was work?" asked Nick.

"Well, you know, work," she rolled her eyes.

"Hi Christine, welcome home," Mary sent her a smile.

"Hey Mary! I didn't know you were coming to visit. Everything okay?"

"That kind of brings us to the latest developments. We will have a family meeting tonight here in the rec room. Mary will stay down here, so we were making it a little more comfortable for her and us. I'll explain after dinner, which I understand is to be down here at our little picnic table," Nick explained.

"Okay, come and help set us up for a camp cookout," Amy announced from the doorway with her arms full of tarp, plastic dishes, and silverware. Everyone clustered around and took one item to add to the picnic. Amy and Christine headed up the stairs to gather food and napkins that they passed to eager hands.

Christine stopped in her bedroom to drop off her briefcase and coat. Soon she joined the others for a plate of hotdogs, potato salad, and fruit. They all had fun and lots of laughs as the kids competed in a contest of who could toss the most grapes into a bowl. After their picnic, they settled down to talk about Mary's boss and what happened today at the house. Davy and Nick walked to the barn to feed the animals, and scanned the woods where Mary said the watcher was hiding earlier.

"He's still there," Nick announced to the group when he returned, "I hope he's freezing out there."

"Okay, Mary, what is this all about?" asked her uncle.

Mary took a deep breath and told them all she knew. "I only know that." she said, "my boss is missing, our Benton location in Houston is on lockdown, and he told me it's important for me to stay free and try to figure out what this is all about."

"Are you sure that all of Benton is on lockdown?"

"The Houston location is locked down, that's what Henry told me. I haven't had time to check for myself. Benton Deep Space Sensing Corporation is global, and if they try to shut all the locations down, people would ask too many questions. I'm worried they might track my cell phone, which is why I threw it away after demolishing it. I kept the memory card from it."

"All right, first things first. Mary, where is your car?" Nick asked.

"I parked it in the ravine by the old cabin."

"Davy, do you remember the space under the floor of the barn used during the Civil War? My thought is we move Mary's car into that space. It's pretty big, so maybe we can also move Mary into it too. That way if those men come back to search the house, they won't find a thing."

"You must tell me the story of how that was used in the Civil War sometime," Mary said.

"But what about the kids?" Mary looked over at the eager, and inquisitive kids who were soaking up everything the adults were saying.

"Oh, don't worry about these two. They can keep a secret, especially when they know that if they don't, they will have to answer to both me, their grandma, their father and mother, and you."

"Aunt Mary, we'll help keep you safe," Mara looked up into Mary's face, tears starting to form in her eyes.

"I know you will," Mary said as she gave the little girl a hug. "Me too," chimed in Jimmy, earning him a hug too.

"Okay, that's settled. Pass me that potato salad," Nick said with a wink to Mara and Jimmy. Davy reached over and hugged his two children.

"Oh, that was good," Mary stretched her arms over her head. She hadn't realized she was so tired. "Oh, sorry," she said, yawning as she gathered the dirty dishes.

"You stay right there, we'll clean up. You have had quite a day, it's no wonder you're tired," Amy told her. "I think Nick has something he wants to discuss with you." she quickly gathered the dishes and with the help of the kids got the dirty dishes and leftover food cleared away.

"Mary, I was thinking about what would happen if you moved into the bolt hole in the barn. I don't think we can just walk over there, not with those men watching the house. Also, don't our cellphones have tracking capability programmed into them too? We all have smartphones."

"Oh dear, I didn't think about them tracking me here. Oh, Uncle Nick, I'm so sorry, I... I didn't..."

"It's okay, don't you worry now. We don't know if they showed up because we are family or if they tracked you. I think now we should do something about it. Davy could go to some nearby towns and purchase some burner phones. And we can remove the memory chips from our phones and destroy the phones. What do you think?"

Mary was silent for a long time as she tried to look at the situation from all angles. Granted, she didn't have any espionage experience, but she had done fieldwork with various government agencies and had listened intently when various agents spoke. The idea her uncle's suggestion made sense, and she wanted to kick herself for overlooking a basic rule if followed by foreign agents. All government employees went through the classes. Benton went through them too, even though they were not technically a government agency.

"Okay, I think we should do it. Anything to make it harder for them to track me, or us, makes sense. Also, I need to figure out what exactly is happening. They are holding my director and my friends; I don't know where he is or why they are holding him. I have some information that Henry wanted to talk about with his friend, then everything started happening after we left his friend's office. Henry thought maybe his friend called someone after we left his office to report our visit."

"Have you read the information he gave you yet?" asked Nick.

"Not yet, I only have a brief idea. Henry said he wanted to protect me, just in case. So, I have been hesitant to read it and, also there is the fact that I really haven't had time."

"Why don't you get some rest and then you can read that information with a clear mind? Davy and I will take care of the cellphones," he said as he gave her a hug, and then left the room.

Chapter 15

Henry Evans laid on his cot, staring at the ceiling. They should at least give you something to read, he thought to himself. He had been in this cell for three days now, with only small breaks for some exercise. He now appreciated anew what prisoners went through. A terrifying thought went through his mind. *What if they didn't let him out, and he was just left to live his life here in this ten by ten-foot space*?

"Want to stay here?" came a voice from behind him. He recognized that voice.

"Hello, Director Cummings. What brings you down here? Slumming? I keep wondering why you have the run of the place and I'm in here," Henry asked.

"You don't have to stay here. Just tell them what they want to know and everything will be all right."

"You really believe that? I don't even know what the hell they want, and I don't believe that everything will be 'all right' as you say."

"You don't need to believe me. They want to speak with you, so come with me."

"Just answer one question, Harold. Are you a traitor to our country? Or just naïve?"

Harold didn't answer, he just opened the cell door and waited while Henry levered himself up off the cot. They moved down the narrow hallway to the stairs leading to his unknown captors.

They only went a short distance to a shower area. There he found clean clothing and toiletries. It was a meager room, but it had what he needed.

"Hey, these are my clothes and things from my hotel room."

"Yes, they brought everything from both your room and your assistant's rooms. Hurry up, he doesn't like to be kept waiting. He has a few questions for you."

"I have a few for him," he responded as he finished his quick shower and was ushered down the hall to an elevator. He tried to take in as much of his environment as possible without being obvious. The elevator had narrow windows where he could see buildings in the distance. He counted floors as they rose above street level. The elevator itself was gleaming metal, but he didn't think it was an elevator used by the public. It had marks on the floor that looked like heavy items had scarred it, like a maintenance elevator. This meeting was being held in secret, even from the other building occupants.

They got off the elevator on the fourth floor and moved down an eerily silent hallway to a large double door guarded by two large men with guns. He wondered what they thought an older two-hundred-pound man could do against two physically fit men. He noticed that Harold stepped aside as the door opened and the two guards ushered him into the suite. Henry still recognized nothing about the room or what building they were in from the little he could see so far. Even the window curtains were drawn. They directed him to sit in the single chair in front of a huge desk. The only other door to the room was on the right of the desk. He looked closely at that desk; it seemed too big for the room, like it had been taken from a larger room to this smaller one.

The man who walked through the door surprised him. He didn't recognize him, but still he held an aura of authority. He was dressed in black, and Henry immediately thought of the famous movie 'Men in Black.' He had always thought of them as fiction, yet his second thought was *what if they exist*?

"Good morning, director." the man mumbled. His voice barely reached Henry's ears.

"Good morning, er… Sorry I didn't catch your name."

"My name is not important, but the information you have is very important. Let us begin. Can you give me a summary of why you went to the Director of ISMC for information and help?"

"I'm sorry, but I can't answer your questions without knowing who you are and where you stand in our national security."

"Come, director, we all work for the same government."

"Do we? Prove it. Tell me who you are and what agency you represent and also why would the United States government lock me, the Director of Benton Deep Space Sensing Corporation in Houston, up for three days?"

"What can I say that would prove it to you? My job, so to speak, is to get you to impart your information to us. We need that information so we can evaluate if our national security is at risk."

"Or, you could be a foreign agent trying to find out what we know. You still haven't told me your name or what agency you work for. Seems like we are at an impasse."

"You may be right. Guards, escort Director Evans back to his cell."

"Can I get something to read? Are they any more people being held? When is lunch served?" All his questions were ignored, but on the way back to his cell he again gathered as much information as he could. His guards had put a cloth sack over his head when they first brought him to his cell, but he could hear and feel that they seemed to travel around corners, always turning to the left so he was sure they always travelled in a circle. There were sounds of traffic and the clack of railroad tracks, but he had not climbed onto a plane or helicopter. This time he could look all around as they ushered him back to his cell and could verify that they had indeed travelled in a circle. Outside his cell, the building looked like a castle of some sort, but he didn't know of any castle-like buildings around Atlanta. His guards were obviously military trained, and they regarded him with a calm indifference and silence. It was unnerving, exactly as it was meant to be. He had a lot to think about. They could keep this up for as long as they wanted, or they could escalate how they dealt with him. They could break him eventually and he would tell them everything, which, granted, was not much. He had asked Harold about tracking a response signal from the one signal they had detected. They must need the location of the original signal that was sent from Earth.

Two days later, they again escorted him back to the office. He decided that this time he needed to go on the offensive.

They again marched into the familiar room with its isolated chair. This time they didn't make him wait; the man was waiting for him.

"Well, have you learned your lesson? Ready to cooperate now?" as the man walked around the desk and closer to the chair.

For the briefest moment, Henry thought the man looked nervous. "I want to know where my people are being kept and what are you doing to them."

"You need not worry about them, just worry about yourself."

"Someone will notice so many people disappearing at once. I worry about them and I need verification that they are okay."

"We put out a story that played on the major television networks that the Benton Deep Space Sensing Corporation operation at that location had to temporary close because of an electronic emergency."

"You can't do that. They pick Benton locations for the global coverage. They are important," Henry sputtered.

"Oh, but we can. Now, let's start again." He rushed around the desk and leaned over Henry. "I have given you every opportunity to answer my questions and you have persisted in this need to know about your people. I will give you one more time to answer me or your people will suffer." He visibly took some time to calm himself.

"I still want to know. Do what you want with me, but I won't do anything until I know that they are not being mistreated." he sat back and crossed his arms.

"Why don't we do this another way? How about talking to Director Cummings?"

"Why don't you just tell me why all the cloak and dagger stuff? I asked one question of Harold and ended up being treated like a criminal."

"Perhaps I didn't make myself clear. Guards, take him back to his cell and show him I mean business."

Henry stood up but stumbled when the guards grabbed his arms and forced him roughly toward the door. Later, he tenderly fingered his cheek where several nice bruises were forming. He wondered how far the guards would go in their persuasions if he continued to refuse. His aches bloomed all over his body as he tried to exercise in the small area of his cell. He did pushups and some jumping jacks to loosen up a bit, then he did some running in place. He knew it might not help a lot. You can't make up for years of not enough activity overnight.

"Ahem, trying to get in shape? I think it might be too late for that," Harold said from the other side of the bars.

Henry ignored him and kept pushing himself to finish his reps. By the time he did, he was out of breath and Harold was still smiling at him from the door.

"Can't you go away? I really don't want to talk with you."

"I need to talk to you," Harold insisted.

"The last time I talked to you, I landed in a cell. What could you possibly say that I would want to hear?"

"We could talk about that shiner you're sporting and how to avoid gaining more of the same."

"Ha-ha, go away."

"Seriously, you don't know this man. I don't know him either, but he is powerful and can do to your people what he is doing to you. Do you want that?"

"This is all unnecessary. I told you everything I know, and you went running to this person. Is he one of the fabled 'men in black?' Harold, what is this really all about?"

"I think he wants more information than what you told me. Do you have more information? He is very serious about getting more out of you."

"What exactly did you tell him?"

"I told him everything you told me. The only thing is, I couldn't swear to him you had told me everything. I guess I'm responsible for you being here. Just tell him what you told me."

"Would he believe me?"

"I don't know."

Chapter 16

The strange men who watched the house varied their locations around the property, but Nick and Davy, in their everyday tasks, always knew where they were hiding. Nick had destroyed the family's cellphones and Davy got new ones from a town called Greenup, a hundred miles away when he went to get some parts for a tractor.

"Aunt Amy, thanks so much for getting me some new clothes. I'm sorry for bringing trouble to you and the family."

"Don't you worry about that." She pinched a good inch of Demin pant and put a pin there. "Have you been losing weight? Some good cooking will do you some good. You're getting skinny," she teased.

"I wanted to lose a little, my clothes were getting too tight because of all the sitting I was doing. Really, I probably should join a gym."

Amy got a dreamy look in her eye as she said, "oh, what I would give for a spa or a back rub."

"Maybe, when this mess is all cleared up, we can go together, all three of us."

"Oh, that would be lovely."

They heard footsteps coming down the stairs, and they both jumped.

"Didn't mean to startle you, it's only us. We have an idea and wanted to run it by you," Nick said as he and Davy walked into the room.

"What is it?" both women said as they became instantly attentive.

"Wait a minute, I need a beer first. Anyone want something to drink? A beer or a soft drink?"

"Okay, thanks Dad, I'll have a beer. Let's sit down so we can talk. Mom or Mary, anything to drink?" Davy asked as he dropped into a chair. They both shook their heads no.

"We were trying to figure out a way to open that space in the barn without arousing the suspicion of our unwanted visitors. We rearranged the space inside the barn to look like we were making room for more animals in there. There is a lot of room in that space under the floor. My great grandfather dug it out just after the Civil War broke out. Kentucky went with the Union, but West Virginia was being fought over by both sides. Virginia had gone with the Confederacy and the Union didn't want to see the newly formed West Virginia go with them too." He stopped to take a sip of his beer.

"We don't need a history lesson," protested Amy.

"Hear me out, I'm getting there. There is a point to all this. In the first year of the war they fought all over the place and it was coming further and further into Kentucky. One day a young soldier stumbled into the barn. He was badly hurt. My great grandfather and great grandmother found him and took care of him night and day. They heard whispers that some Confederate soldiers were in the woods looking for a Union soldier. Kentucky in those days was teetering back and forth between North and South and some people would have turned him over to the Confederate soldiers. They decided that they would hide him in the barn, but they were afraid the soldiers would easily find him. So, they dug a root cellar and covered it with hay in a vacant stall. They enlarged the root cellar over time and used it to hold other runaways. I think we can use that for you, Mary. Davy and I work in the barn all the time and we wouldn't have to worry if these men searched the house or the barn. What do you think?"

"It's not fancy, but I think we could make it comfortable for you," Davy added.

"Great, how can I help?"

"I'm surprised you're so enthusiastic."

"Just give me my papers, lots of blank paper, lots of pens and my phone. I'll be fine. Besides, I love that old barn with its rafters so high up in the air. Poetic, isn't it?"

"Okay, hold on now, we still have to get you over to the barn, and before that, get your new home cleaned up and re-built a little," Davy laughed as he gave her a little shove, which she promptly returned. "And we already put your car down there."

"All right, kids. You're grown up now," Nick admonished, smiling.

"When do we start?" Mary asked.

"Immediately."

The next day, Nick started by moving bundles of hay and cleaning the floor on one side of the barn. Davy went into town to buy the wood needed for building the stalls. They planned on three new stalls along one wall. Meanwhile, Mary and Amy started gathering things Mary might need or enjoy. When they were sure no one was looking, they worked on the secret room.

Nick and Davy were both surprised when men came striding into the barn.

"What are you doing on my land?" Nick demanded as he rolled up the plans they had been looking over.

Davy moved toward the pitchfork hanging on the wall.

"I wouldn't do that if I were you," one of the men said.

"Don't you dare threatened me," Davy took an angry step toward the man.

"People, stand down," ordered the man who seemed to be the leader.

"And why, pray tell, should we stand down? We do not want you here, and this is my land. You and your goons need to leave or I will call our sheriff and file trespassing charges," Nick said in a quiet voice. Davy gave him a startled look and backed up a few steps, he knew what that voice meant.

"That wouldn't do you any good. Now, we need to know what you are doing out here."

"What, why? This is my property and you have no right to march in here demanding to know what we are doing. Why are you here?"

"Yes, why are you here?" said Amy, who stood in the doorway with Christine holding guns on the intruders. "The man asked a very good question, and I have a few more to add. One – why are you here? Two – where's your identification? And three – do you know what trespassing is?"

"One – we have important matters to discuss, two – you don't need to see our identification, and three – we can go wherever we want."

"Why are you arguing with them? They can't even shoot those things," one of the men jeered.

"Try me," said Christine, as she fired a warning shot toward the feet of the leader.

"Boss, let me teach that bitch some respect."

"Button it, you gave her a chance to prove she could shoot, and she took it."

"I think it's time for you men to leave. I won't ask again," Amy said. "And just to be clear, no one comes on our land and threatens my family," she gestured with the gun toward the door, "and next time, if there is a next time, call first. We have a large farm to run here, in case you didn't notice."

They all followed the men out of barn and down to the road where the SUVs waited. Nick and Davy stood proudly behind their wives.

"They should know better than to go against the Grand Champion Sharpshooter of Greenup county," Davy teased his wife.

"From now on, we don't leave the house without a gun," Nick said with a frown.

Chapter 17

While Davy teased his wife about her skills in sharpshooting, the black SUVs moved down the road about a mile and then pulled to the side. Several men were still griping about being outmaneuvered, but the leader had bigger things on his mind.

Nehemit, leader of the containment specialists, became concerned that it was taking too long to find the female. They had traced her to this farm, but had not found her as yet. Their chief administrator would be furious with this delay. Nehemit signaled to one of the men and moved a little away from the others. The man hurried over and handed him an item that looked like a two-way transmitter, but was infinitely more powerful. He momentarily wondered if any of the other team leaders had run into trouble with their assignments, then dismissed the thought. The chief had the habit of getting rid of anyone who didn't produce. He just had to make sure he wasn't one of them.

"Chief Administrator, this is Nehemit, reporting. We are on the trail of the only other person who had contact with the man from Benton Deep Space Sensing Corporation. That asset is being detained and talking to the leader of their ISMC government group. So far, it has been easy to get them to work with us and we will have full containment soon. We are accepted here as a shadow government group that goes by the name of 'men in black.' We will report again in six Earth hours."

Nehemit knew that each group leader would send their own carefully worded reports to the chief, who carefully kept each captain separate from each other. *Earthlings are so stupid*, he thought, *considering how the chief used that separation to helped him hide the activities of his operatives,*

Moments later, on the planet Tottahagan, the chief administrator sat back in his chair with a smile on his face. His plans were progressing better than he thought they would. Earthlings were unwary and unsure of life outside of their own small interests. His plans to take the elements he needed from them to make his own laser cannons was going well. Rehe, his agent in charge of getting those elements, had reported that his men had gotten the needed amount of two of the elements from the locations in the country of India. Rehe reported that India had terrible security on those mines for Ytterbium and Europium. The other needed element, Terbium, would soon be in their hands. He laughed gleefully as he indulged himself in his dream of blowing up a planet as they pleaded for his mercy, offering him anything he wanted. Maybe he would blow up the puny Earth, he thought, as he laughed and danced around the room. He just had to keep those pesky Maveners from knowing what he was doing on Earth.

Meanwhile, in orbit around Earth, the People's drone recorded all transmissions sent by Tottahagan operatives out into space. It then sent all transmissions back to the hub for decoding.

Chapter 18

In the center, Zebut had directed the drone to fly down the middle of the projected cone he had circling around his head. The messages from the missing drone had told them that there were men dressed all in black interfering and tampering with the people who had rescued it from its geode prison. Zebut was sure it was a raiding party from the planet Tottahagan. His people had negotiated with their government before in order to maintain peace in their area of space. Tottahagan did not give in easily. The treaty was a hard-won prize for all the settled planets in that parsec. That species, unfortunately, seemed to believe any planet not as developed as theirs, was by rights, a legitimate target.

The People's agents had filed a report summarizing the suspected actions by Tottahagan citizens in violation of their treaty. The governing board called the Council of Planets, made up of representatives from all the advanced civilizations in this area of space, had stipulated that Zebut find which planet the reports were coming from and send aid.

The People did not believe in violence, but they had been experienced enough to achieve their objectives by other means. Zebut debated on which means would be most effective in this case. He studied how they handled past troubles. He read of many methods used to control Tottahagan's violations in the past. First, he needed to make sure it was definitely Tottahagans committing the violations. Evidence came in many forms and one of them was a firsthand series of intercepted messages to the Tottahagan planet from agents on the planet Earth's surface. Next, he needed the drone to confirm that Tottahagan agents were responsible. Zebut looked at the original message and ordered that it show the region it came from, and highlight the planet it came from, known by its people as Earth. The drone that Zebut had order to travel to the area of space that the old drone had sent its messages from reported that it had just entered that planetary system.

"Send message acknowledging entering system and ask for a situation update," Zebut ordered. Satisfied that the drone would report back, Zebut dictated a report, summarizing his reasoning and the course of action he planned to pursue. He also made note of his objectives to prove that it was his opinion that Tottahagan was committing the violations by providing the firsthand evidence. He could plan no action until he had solid proof.

The drone signaled that it was in a parking orbit between the fourth planet and the asteroid belt. Zebut ordered it to report any messages being sent from the planet Earth to Tottahagan and make a recording of it. He thought it wouldn't take long because their agents loved to brag about their exploits, hoping to get more projects.

"Signal me if any report comes from either of the drones." Zebut requested.

Zebut's day had finally ended, and he was looking forward to a quiet dinner and time with his wife. He travelled down three levels in the hub to the apartments of current workers. Tor-Kon Mar also worked in the hub, so they were lucky. She worked as an Astro-analyst, analyzing the position and make-up of the stars, while his title was Senior Signal Evaluator for the drone project.

Their residence was a large but compact space that suited them perfectly. It had two bedrooms, communal area and a workroom. All spaces in the center had floors that automatically formed tables, chairs, and any other special shapes as needed. The room provided a hominess by use of color, shape or texture. A simple request could achieve these. Zebut liked the privacy the bedrooms gave them, even though the floor could have formed a bed in the communal space. This way his wife could sleep longer and he wouldn't wake her up if he needed to work.

Mar had beaten him home by ten minutes and had dinner ready. The aroma reached him as soon as he walked in the door. His stomach growled, which made his wife hide a smile.

"Smells delicious, I am starving. Thank you for making dinner," he said as they exchanged bows.

"I wondered if you would be home tonight. You have been working long hours lately," Mar said.

"Yes, I am tired, but I wanted to spend some time with you. You also have been very busy. Can you tell me about what you are doing?" he asked, knowing that sometimes her work was classified.

"Yes, I can! It is very exciting because we have found another galaxy. Our investigation of it is just at the beginning, but there are so many star systems out there, it's exciting to add to our knowledge." she laughingly told him with her eyes sparkling.

"That is very exciting, but I hope it won't keep you away from me often," he teased her as he tenderly rubbed her shoulder.

"Nothing will keep me away from you for very long, my love," she answered as she turned to wrap her forearm around his and kissed his knuckles.

A soft chime sounded and he moved to answer the summons to the message being sent on his communication unit. The message made him raise his eyebrows in surprise as he read the three transcripts. He quickly ordered the message appended to his notes regarding Tollahagan. When he finished, he stood still in contemplation of the added impact of the new information.

Mar watched him and noticed how his shoulders slumped and then straightened. She smiled as she saw him think the information through and then accept his responsibility in the matter. She didn't know what information he had read, but she knew her husband. He was a resolute and fair man, and he would face whatever consequences came his way. She was so proud of him and loved him passionately.

"Let's eat, my love."

He turned to her, smiling. He also knew his wife and her talent for taking care of him. He also loved her deeply.

Chapter 19

Annette busied herself with making something to eat for everyone while Dan and Tom tried to move debris out of the way. This was doubly hard when they were trying to stay out of Annette's way and out of view of anyone who might look in the windows, but they soon had the debris stacked and a path cleared enough that Annette could move around easier in the kitchen. They had leaned the backdoor pieces up as well as they could, and put a chair in front to hold it there. She missed her crafts, but the excitement of trying to outwit the bad guys beat glass fusing or crocheting any day. Annette kept thinking of the fused glass pieces she would make when she got home, especially based on her adventures she was having right now.

"Should I call the police and report those men, or would that only bring more attention to the house?" Annette turned worried eyes on the men in the kitchen. "I'm worried that I should report to them, as that would be what I would normally do, and if I don't do that, that might bring questions."

"I propose that you should do what you would normally do. We can hide downstairs while the police are here," Dan said.

"I think that's wise, but Annette, it is up to you. If it worries you that they might catch us here, we can leave. That way you would be safe. We don't want to jeopardize that," Tom added.

"But you can't go home. Your house is in the same shape as this one," she argued. "But, thanks for the offer anyway, and I do appreciate the sentiment. To tell the truth, I feel safer with all of you here, and we can't let them capture any of you, especially Pebble."

"No, we can't go home. That would lead to too many questions. I think we can chance the closet."

"Okay, we'll go with that decision. Let me go do that now, before I lose my courage." She hurried out of the room.

Dan and Tom headed downstairs to tell the others of the decision. Quickly they scanned the room for any telltale traces of them being there. Then they waited, it didn't take long for the police to arrive. They could barely hear what was being said through the layers inside the closet.

"Thank you for coming officer. It has been quite a fright," Annette gushed to the policeman.

"Mrs. Cunningham, can you describe what happened here?"

She quickly told him about her interactions with the men dressed in black leaving out only the parts concerning the group hiding in the downstairs closet.

"That's a lot of food there. Are you expecting company?"

Annette turned stricken eyes on all the food. "Oh no," she moaned, "the food. It's been sitting out too long. It's all ruined. I was trying to fill the freezer for my daughter and her husband so they wouldn't have to fix anything when they got home. Now, they will come home to a mess and no food in the freezer to eat." she turned vengeful eyes on the police officer.

"You find them and put them in jail." And she broke down in tears.

"Yes, ma'am, we'll do our best. Just a few more questions and we'll get out of your hair. Did they touch anything, maybe they left prints?"

"No, they had gloves on. They wore all black and drove black SUVs. Sorry officer, I really wish I could be more helpful," she answered his question in sobs.

"Any help is appreciated. We will take photographs of the damage for our records, so if you see someone taking pictures, don't panic. You might want to take pictures too, to give to your daughter and son-in-law for insurance purposes."

"Okay, I'll do that. I need to take care of this food." Annette got busy with the food, but she kept an alert eye on all the people rummaging through the house. She jumped when the officer asked her to come downstairs. He was standing by the fireplace, staring at the board in his hands.

"Yes, officer?"

"What is this?" he said, holding the board out to her.

"Oh, that? If you look in the space behind where the board was, you'll see the gas meter. Isn't it clever? My son-in-law came up with that. That meter was right there, looking like a complete eyesore. He built the surround and enclosed the meter, but he had to make it so the meter reader could get to it to read it. I thought it was a brilliant solution. Don't you?"

"Yes, ma'am, but it made me jump when it came out. Let me put this back and then we can get out of your hair."

"You are a dear. Thank you for all your help, Officer."

After the police left, Annette hurried back downstairs to let everyone know that they left. They didn't need an update from Annette because they heard everything that had been said. What they wanted to see was the clever solution her son-in-law created for the gas meter. Annette had a grand time showing them the catch to release the wood panel. Then they all settled down to eat and discuss what to do now.

Pebble was lying quietly in Jenny's hand as they listened to the adults discuss what to do next when it got that tingling feeling again. It was getting another message. "Entering planetary system. What is your status?" It looked up to see everyone staring at it.

"What's wrong?" Tom asked.

"Another message." It repeated it word for word. "What is my status?" it asked.

"Okay, lets send our status and -" Tom trailed off when Jenny pulled on his elbow. "What is it, honey?"

"I have an idea," said Jenny.

"You do?" Tom asked, surprised because she had been so quiet, he had almost forgotten she was there.

"Mommy and I were reading about space and the book said that there were thousands of things orb...orbiting around our planet. What if the drone could be just another thing orbiting?"

"Jenny, you are a genius!" exclaimed Tom as he picked up his daughter and twirled her around the room. "Pebble, can you tell the drone to enter earth orbit and blend with all the objects? Tell it to do a natural-looking orbit. And tell it what is happening now."

"Yes, Tom." Pebble was quiet for a minute. "Message sent and acknowledged by the drone. I also told it about the bad men in black."

"Good." he paused, trying to think if he missed anything, but nothing came to mind. "Those were excellent ideas, Pebble and Jenny, you make a great team, but we still need to decide what to do next. We can't stay here. Annette, however much we would like to stay, we still have to find a way out of this mess." he stared at his hands for a minute. "How about Malinda and Dan go back to work, they might have better luck running interference for us from there?"

Dan opened his mouth to protest, but slowly closed it again as he thought about the idea. "That might work, as long as you four don't get in hot water."

Tom glanced at his wife and child. He abhorred that they would be on the run. Jenny had school she was missing and Colleen was pregnant. There didn't seem to be any other alternatives they could make. As for Pebble, it wanted to stay with Jenny and that meant Tom and Colleen would insist on coming too.

"Well, as long as the drone can continue to orbit unde-tected, it gains us some time," said Malinda into the silence. "Is there anyone else we can contact to help?"

"How about the Benton Deep Space Sensing Corporation office in California? We know they have shut down the Hous-ton office, but maybe the California office would have more information?" Dan asked.

"How would you contact us to keep us informed? I need a new phone, one that is untraceable, like a burner phone. An-nette, I hate to ask you, but could you get ones for all of us?" Malinda asked, turning to Annette.

"That should be easy enough. I have some shopping to do, so I'll get them then."

The next day, Annette made her trips to the home im-provement store at a local shopping center to get some items to help repair the house and replacements for some broken house plants. She also went to the grocery store that was also right there to replace the spoiled food. While she was there, she stopped and filled up the gas tank on the car. No one paid any attention to the fact that she also got the burner phones, laughing that her grandchildren could call her when she had to return home. She also hurried into a department store for a gift for a friend. When she returned from her shopping, she had a grand time with Jenny planning where to put the new, pretty pots of flowers around the house with Pebble adding its opinion. She packed care packages of food for everyone to take with them, and she filled the freezer full of delicious dishes for her daughter and her son-in-law. But her eyes filled with tears as she gave her goodbyes to all her new friends. Even Pebble rubbed her cheek and purred when it was its turn to say goodbye.

"Take care and stay safe," she said as she waved them on their way. She turned and looked at the house and remembered how excited she had been to be by herself for a while with the only thing to do was watch the house and crochet. *Look at me now*. she thought. *Bored already, and they have only been gone a few minutes. Well, one thing I can do is call someone to fix the back door and the damage to the kitchen.* And she did that with a satisfying grin as she thought how surprised her daughter would be when she got home and her kitchen had that island she had been wanting.

Chapter 20

The People's drone had sent an update of the latest message from the planet. It made all the course corrections as ordered. It had even complied with the request from the older drone and settled into an undetected orbit around the planet as it attached itself to an satellite in orbit. It wondered what it was all about. When the People, as all the drones called them, had given them artificial intelligence, all the drones had thought about the worlds they saw and the wonders of the universe. There it waited for either another message from the older drone or an order from its people. It also recorded messages from Tottahagan agents on Earth, specifically from lands called India and United States of America to the Chief Administrator on Tottahagan. It sent all recorded messages to Maven.

Zebut read the messages and sent them on to his superiors. He was surprised to receive a summons to come down the space elevator to the administration building. He walked through quiet halls until he reached the elevator, but he sent a message to let his wife know and so packed a light pack in case he needed to stay the night. He loved riding the elevator down to the surface of the planet, but it was a long descent. He could take the teleport, but the ride on the elevator gave him such a magnificent all-around view during the four-hour ride down the slender support. He always thought it great fun to start in the darkness of space and slowly slide through the layers of atmosphere and into the brightness of the sun shining down, as it was now, or if he descended at night, into the darkness that was only broken by the twinkling lights of cities with their gleaming pseudo-glass spirals. It was breathtaking, and he loved it.

Four hours later, he stepped off the elevator on the second highest floor of the two hundred story Space Administration building. He hurried down hallways made from the pseudo-glass where he could see down through the floor and out the windows surrounding him on the spiraling side. If he looked at the building from outside, it looked like a strand of DNA, winding around a central axis. The rooms on the outside of the central axis were opaque for privacy, but at a touch of a button or voice command could be made transparent. Occasionally, designs adorned the spiraling walkway or side walls, representing trees, flowers, or vines. He could also change the designs themselves at a voice command. Zebut thought it was all lovely.

Zebut soon arrived at his destination. He walked through the door and presented himself to the welcoming computer by giving it his name and who he wanted to speak with. The room welcomed him, and knowing his preferences, turned a lovely shade of blue and served a tall glass of his favorite drink. A very comfortable table and chair combination formed out of the floor, and Zebut sat down and prepared himself to wait.

While he waited, the computer occasionally asked if he was comfortable or if he needed his drink refreshed. He asked if it could play soft music while he waited. He was engaged in ordering his thoughts for the coming meeting, when a soft chime sounded. The computer thanked him and displayed a map showing him the route. He bowed as he left the room and moved once again into the hallway. This time he moved to the inner edge of the spiral where an escalator moved up the hallway a little way to a juncture where Zebut grabbed a handhold and turned left into another office. He again presented himself, but this time a woman rose to greet him.

"Zebut, how nice to see you again," she said as she bowed and smiled up at him.

"It is always my pleasure to see you, Councilor Aeolus." He smiled and bowed in return.

"Have a seat and tell me about this little drone you have found," she said as she sat herself on a seat that formed for her and him from the floor.

"I really think the drone found us. It is a fascinating story. I have all the reports between our drone that is patrolling, and some of the reports from the older drone. There is a gap because the older drone either stopped sending reports or could not send reports for a significant amount of time. We haven't been able to find that out yet because we believe the planet is being interfered with by our friends from Tottahagan. If it is them, they are in violation of the treaty, but it might be a rogue group causing problems."

"What is the position of our patrolling drone?"

"It has positioned itself on one of the asteroids in a far orbit around their planet. It can stay in touch with the drone that is on the planet and send reports to us."

"What is the planet's level of development?" asked the Councilor.

"It is at Level A-10. It has achieved space travel within its system and has pockets of mining in their asteroid belt. It also has some tentative settlement development on their moon and one planet in their system. They still divide the planetary population into countries, some of which are hostile to each other. I think if we remain vigilant, we will see in one or two thousand years that they will either destroy themselves or will learn to work together."

The Councilor thought for a moment as she weighed all the facts and options. "My recommendation is that we take action to remove the agents from Tottahagan as discretely as possible and issue their government a warning. Let them decide what to do with them. Try to keep our involvement to a minimum, although we may need to have the older drone testify as to the involvement of Tottahagan agents. We can retrieve the older drone or if it wants, it can stay, but must remain silent about its origins, if possible. We can monitor that part of space, but no direct contact until they are ready. Now that business is done, are you staying the day in the city? You have been so busy, your father and I hardly see you anymore," the Councilor asked with a polite bow as she rose.

"I would like to visit, at least for a day or two. Unfortunately, Mar cannot join us. She is in the midst of a very exciting project. Thank you, Mother, for all your help."

"We will miss her. Would you like to meet for dinner? Your father also would enjoy seeing you, and, of course, you will stay with us during your visit."

"Yes, I would like that." he bowed to his mother and affectionately kissed her cheek.

Zebut again moved to the escalator and rode it down to street level. The transporter was available, but he liked to walk, especially in the city with the unfiltered air and parks. He wanted to buy some clothing for tonight's dinner. As he walked down the street, he noticed some stores he wished he had more time to stop and browse, but he had a mission. He had been on duty when his parents had observed their anniversary and he wanted to get them something special. He finally found what he wanted for them. It was a painting done in the beautiful shades of blue and green and some colors he couldn't even name, which formed continuous circles of random patterns. He hoped that they would like it.

He stepped into the shop and approached the shopping screen. He hit the scan button for products and looked for the painting he wanted. *Good, I can afford that*, he thought in relief. He then hit the pay and wrap buttons and selected an appropriate greeting to go with it while he waited for his purchase to be prepared. His package arrived in a few minutes and he made arrangements for it to be sent to his parents' residence.

Smiling, he left the store. On down the street, he came to his favorite store for most of his clothing.

"Hello, again. Are you here for something special?" said the sales clerk as she bowed.

"Yes, thank you for your help," he said as he also bowed and told her what he wanted.

"Please step this way." she turned and walked toward a viewing tube.

He followed her and stepped into the tube. "I want some formal dress clothes and another set of my work clothes."

She pressed two buttons, and he saw himself in his work clothes. He was about to say that was fine, when she pressed another button and the clothes that he was wearing in the screen changed subtly. He liked the slight color change and fit even better, but he asked, "are these regulation clothes okay for me to wear for work?"

"Yes, the new design just came in and a lot of our customers find them very pleasing, especially the fact that the color changes enhance each different skin tone."

"Yes, I do too. I would like to have three sets, please. Now, what do you have that is dress formal?"

Later, he walked out of the shop thrilled with his purchases, which he had sent to his family's home.

Chapter 21

The director was resting on his cot when he heard the now familiar footsteps approaching his cell. He wondered how long they would continue to keep him here. It seemed like too much trouble to get up, so he closed his eyes and pretended to sleep.

"So, we're pretending to sleep now, are we?" said the familiar voice.

"Why not? You have nothing that I want to hear."

"Even if I came to tell you that you are free to go?" teased the smug voice.

"Funny, I don't hear the jangle of keys."

The sound of keys turning and the creak of a rusty door had the director opening his eyes and looking toward the door. "What's the catch?"

"No catch, you asked me to help you get out of here. I owe you one, so here I am paying you back. Now, we're even."

"I don't think so, I'm not out of here yet. What's the deal? I step out of the cell door and get shot for escaping?"

"You watch too much TV, or maybe you read too many crime novels. Come on, we're wasting valuable time," Harold said as he glanced nervously down the corridor.

"Okay, I'm coming. Anything is better than the monotony of this cell," the director rolled off the cot and followed Harold down the corridor. A couple of feet down the hallway, Harold stopped and pulled out a key which he used to open a hidden door that the director didn't remember seeing before. It surprised the director, when they got to the other side of it, to see trees and shrubberies. They crouched behind some bushes where they could see the gate through which a road ran. Harold pointed to the left and took a passage that ran along the wall. The director looked longingly back toward the road, but Harold headed the other way.

Henry studied the architecture of the building as they ran. He realized that it looked like a medieval castle. He knew he was in America, but where? It was like a medieval castle, but it wasn't Disneyland or Disney World. This one looked like it had been abandoned and it would be easy for these men in black to commandeer it for their use. He hurried after Harold. He was also surprised to find a car waiting for them four blocks down from the castle. The driver had a walkie-talkie on which he was getting surveillance reports. As soon as the two of them were in the car and covered by a blanket on the floor of the back seat, the car moved away and blended with traffic.

They drove through city traffic and into the surrounding area on the other side of town. Only then were they told they could sit.

"Sir, there has been no sign of a chase or alert going out. Reports on all exits report the same thing. The drop off location is coming up on the right, and then I have to get my cousin's car back to him after I clean off the license plate."

"Thanks for your and your cousin's help. We really appreciate it. Stay safe."

Soon, the director found himself walking up a dirt road to what looked like a barn falling down from neglect. The closer they got to it, the more the director noticed odd items lying around on the ground. Leaning against the rickety wood fence was a dilapidated TV antenna, and over by an old well was a tube sticking up against its brick siding. When they walked into the barn itself, they could see horse tack and hay, but one corner had steps going up to a second floor. Instead of going up, Harold pushed a halter out of the way and a section of floor, hay and all, swung up revealing steps going down. The director saw people manning stations and a TV surveillance console working off to the side of the steps.

"Why the secrecy?" he asked Harold.

"This facility is a holdover from early ISMC when we were paranoid about Russian spies. We were trying so hard to beat them in outer space and we were way behind. They had already put a monkey into space and were getting ready to put a man into space. We built and equipped this place and worked our butts off to carry out President Kennedy's promise. Soon we outgrew this place and moved into a much larger location. I thought of this place as soon as you were detained. We need to know what's going on here. I can't find out if these operatives are ours or someone else's masquerading as ours. No one is talking."

"You played your part well, I was convinced. Now, any ideas how to find out which side they are on?"

"Not a clue yet."

"Here are the reports you asked for, sir. Can I get you something to drink or eat?" Harold's assistant asked both of them.

"Do we have sandwiches and maybe a beer? I missed my nightly beer," Henry asked with a smile on his face. He hadn't smiled since his dinner with Mary days ago.

"Let's eat in the lunchroom, it's back this way and I can answer some of your questions," Harold said as he led the way. The installation was much larger than the director noticed at first. There were rooms for planning, gyms, and meetings. Further away from the monitors and equipment, he noticed restrooms, showers for men and women, and dark rooms for naps. Finally, they reached the lunchroom, but even that surprised him. It had a full gleaming kitchen, big enough a five-star chef would be right at home.

"I see I should have asked for more money when we set up Benton in Houston."

"I don't know if you would get what was built here, but I'm glad we got it. Let's sit here and talk about our plans."

"Where is 'here'?"

"We are right outside of Evanston, Illinois. The place you were being held is an abandoned mansion built it in 1927."

Harold pulled out a map of the nation and some paper and pens. "Okay, let's make a list of what we know."

"You know more than I do. I've been in a cell for the last week."

"You might know more than you think. You already told me about the signal, but do you remember anything special about that signal? For example, do you know the direction of the signal, or what area of space it came from?"

"I could tell its inbound trajectory was targeted to a very narrow area in the United States, that's why I came asking if ISMC had a way of tracking a return signal. We tracked it as it travelled in this direction," he said as he drew a line across the map, from west to east, stopping in middle of Ohio.

"You really can track the signal that closely?"

"You track signals to specific locations in space, such as a mining colony. It's the same principal, just in reverse. What we can't do is trace a response signal from earth to outer space. We get thousands of signals from outer space every day; which is a really noisy place. We pick up FRBs (Fast Radar Bursts) every day; but this one was different in that it was not a generalized FRB with a very wide bandwidth. This signal was very tight with a narrow bandwidth. Trying to look at all those signals individually would take more manpower than we have, so we have an algorithm to help separate out the important or the more interesting signals. This signal fell into both categories."

Their lunch arrived, and both men dug in. "Man, I didn't realize I was so hungry," Harold said as he crunched his sandwich. There was no answer from the director, who leaned back and sipped his beer with closed eyes. Harold finished his sandwich and leaned back to enjoy his own beer. Yep, he thought, just right.

"I have a burner phone for you. I know they took away your cellphone, so this can replace that. Do you know of any phone number for someone you can trust to call? We need to let your people know you're okay," supplied Harold as he wiped his chin.

"I have an idea about that. I only put the numbers of my co-workers on my cellphone. I memorized the personal numbers of a few of my co-workers. I thought maybe I could call one of them at home and have them spread the word verbally."

"Let's do it. Do you know which one to try?"

"Yes, I want to try the wife of my signal processing manager, Dr. Alex Meyer. His wife's name is Beth. Alex is a bundle of nerves as they are awaiting their first child. He has Beth call him every day to let him know that she's okay. So, if she calls, it shouldn't raise questions."

"Okay, let's call her."

"Wait, a moment. So, I take it none of my staff is still being held? Can you guarantee that?"

"As far as I know, they are at their stations, but not working."

"So, they are being held. Can they come and go as they please, or are they sleeping there?"

"I was told that they can go home at night, but they need to come into work every day. I assume so they could keep an eye out to see if another signal comes in."

"I want my staff safe. I don't want them to go through what I went through."

"I promise you, to the best of my knowledge, they are safe. Other than that, you know as much as I do."

"Okay, let's call her."

"That's strange," he announced as he clicked the cellphone off. "A recording came on saying that number had been disconnected. I'm sure I remembered it correctly."

Chapter 22

Mary was finally in her new underground home in the barn. She marveled at the cleverness in the use of the space. They filtered fresh air into the space by exploiting the fan system already in use up in the main barn that brought fresh air from outside to freshen the air inside the barn. The space was roomy enough to hold two families, with room for a kitchen, eating area, and two couches. It also had enough space for her car. She also found books for all age levels to read and an exercise bike. The only downside was the loneliness. She hoped that she wouldn't need to be down here that long. The hours of nothing to do allowed her too much time to worry about the director and her co-workers.

She spent a lot of time reading and re-reading the papers from the director's briefcase, hoping to learn something new. Again, she read, then stopped as she thought maybe she was looking at the information on the pages in the wrong way. The director had the habit of writing little notes in the margins of the pages. She had already read them, but didn't really see their importance. Now she started again, making her own notes on the implications of what he wrote in the margins.

The report was a collection of reports from each station in the hub, with the FRB signal highlighted. She started by marking down the page and passage, then the director's note; taking her time to think about the meaning behind each notation. When she got to the part when the signal had only appeared once, the director's note said, "a fluke, or a really targeted signal?" She knew it was normal for signals to repeat, especially if it was from a pulsar which sent out regular beats of electromagnetic radiation. Sometimes team members would scan for a signal for months in order not to miss a repeating signal. She continued to read to glean any more mention of signals.

She got to another page and read that after two hours, the signal had not repeated. It also seemed targeted because it came in on a very narrow bandwidth. Henry had made a large star next to that entry and the word "targeted." She kept reading and finally came to the end of the report. She found one name: "Harold?"

Harold, or Director Harold Cummings of the International Space Mining Corporation (ISMC), was the person they had traveled to see. Right after that meeting strange men followed them and they finally ended up separating, with her traveling to her uncle's house. She had thought of trying to get home to her parent's farm in Wyoming, but her uncle lived closer. Her guess was that they had taken the director against his will by either the government or the strange men they had run from.

She had many friends at the Benton center, but she hesitated to call them. She didn't know if they also were being watched or threatened.

"Hey, down there. You ready to go for a walk?" Davy called down to her.

"Boy, am I! I'm going crazy from boredom. I'm making progress, but it's slow going."

"Then let's go. We toured the whole farm and saw nothing. Dad even put up some hunting cameras. He wanted to do that anyway, to protect the animals from predators. We have some black bears moving into the area."

"Black bear, really?"

"Yeah, more numbers of black bear are moving into Kentucky and Ohio. The cameras are working and already we have seen bears up around the outer pastures. Let's get going or we'll lose the light."

Mary stood breathing deeply of the fresh air. The air down in her small home was fresh, but it wasn't the same as taking it in while outdoors.

Davy handed her the reins of her favorite mare and they mounted up. Mary seemed to glow as she followed Davy away from the barn.

"I missed this," she said as she patted her horse's neck and she saw the flick of the filly's ears in answer.

"At least it's a beautiful day, a good day for a ride, and good exercise for the horse. They get little exercise these days." he patted his handsome gelding.

Together, they walked their horses to the path into the woods, then they moved into a canter, appreciating the cool air under the trees. Mary knew the paths on the farm like the back of her hand, but she was willing to let Davy lead. She felt a little nervous after all they had gone through earlier. Soon, she noticed that Davy was leading them to the pastures used by the wild horses.

"Why are we going this way?" she whispered to Davy, looking around warily.

"I want to see if anyone or anything has messed with dad's cameras. I have my suspicions about our unwanted friends."

Davy dismounted and lead his horse to a little grove of trees that would provide them cover. Mary matched his movements and waited for him to explain. She mouthed the word "why?" and he pointed to the camera on a nearly tree. He knelt down and drew a diagram in the dirt, marking two trees with x's. She looked over where the other camera should be and saw it was gone and the thick strap that had held the camera was cut straight across. Someone had taken the camera. Davy led his horse out of the little thicket and remounted. Mary followed his lead.

"We have to head back so we can tell Dad someone is taking our cameras. I'm sorry Mary, you're not safe after all."

"I'd rather know that I'm not safe, than think I am and get taken by surprise."

"Let's let the horses run, it might be the last real exercise they get for a while."

The horses didn't need any additional urging, and they raced back to the barn. By the time they got there they were out of breath, but not sweaty. Davy and Mary wiped them down and gave them their grain and fresh hay. Mary took her filly's face into her hands and gave her a gentle kiss on her nose. Davy laughed because Mary and her horse had always had a special bond, and it made him happy to see that it still existed. He gave his horse an extra pat too.

Mary returned to her little home away from home, and Davy went to talk with his dad, who he found in his office, looking at this month's expenses.

"Boy, I will have to cut your rations this month," Nick teased his son, and he looked at his face and put the papers to the side. "What's wrong?"

Davy hated having to tell his dad that those men were back. "Someone cut and took one camera from around the wild horse pastures. Mary and I had gone for a ride because she needed to get fresh air. Now she's in danger again. I almost wish someone had been there so I could have winged him."

"I know how you feel, but it would only complicate things more. Our priority is keeping the family safe. Maybe they took it to make us make a bad move."

"Maybe we can get a drone?" Davy suggested.

"That's not a bad idea, but I don't know what the range is, maybe you can research it? The other thing we can do is get more cameras that can be put in the tree canopy and angled down. They might not expect that."

Davy felt better with something concrete he could do to address the situation. "Okay, see you later with my research. It shouldn't take long." He headed up to his room and his computer to begin his research. First, he researched drones, their capabilities and range. Then, he got busy looking up cameras that mounted high in the trees. He worked until dinner and then continued until around eight o'clock at night.

He came downstairs with pages of research to show his dad, who he found in the kitchen talking to his mom and his wife. "Look at her," he said to his wife as he gave her a kiss. "You get prettier every day," he said as he put his hands over his heart.

"Go on with you," she chuckled as she gave him a hug and pinch. "Is Mary coming?"

"Well, that's something we need to talk to you and Mom about. Mary and I went for a ride to get her some fresh air and exercise. We found that someone had stolen one of our cameras up by the wild horse pastures. We think our unwanted friends are back."

"Oh, poor Mary. Someone should stop those people before they do some real harm," Amy said.

"Speaking of Mary, I have been meaning to ask her if she remembered any phone numbers of some of her friends she could call to let them know she's okay."

"Is that wise with those men prowling around the property?" asked Amy.

"Well, she is in the bunker in the barn, and is armed. I don't think there is anything else we can do except keep a close watch. One solution Davy and I thought of was to get some cameras to put up high in the trees around the wild horse pastures and one in the barn. We lost a camera we put on a tree around the wild horse pastures. They just cut it off the tree. Also, Davy suggested a drone. What did you find out?"

"Well, it's a little confusing. Drones come in all sizes and capabilities and prices. Also, they are hard to fly in tree cover, and they are noisy. I think we should try the cameras first. If need be, we could try a drone later."

"What do all of you think?" Nick asked everyone. "I really don't want to call in the sheriff. Hopefully Mary has some phone numbers we can try at least, let someone know she is all right."

"Cameras are okay and phone numbers from Mary," approved Amy.

"I agree," said Christine.

"Okay, I'll go talk to Mary about phone numbers and we'll see about the cameras," Nick got up and move to the door.

When he got to the barn, he started cleaning up, just in case he was being watched. He moved around and checked the horses, picked up halters and also kept a lookout before he headed down to see Mary.

"I'm glad I recognize your walk, or I would have used this." Mary put the shovel down next to the door.

"I just came to let you know what we did about our visitors. You already know about the camera, so we wanted to let you know we will get new ones that will be harder for them to remove, and we are going to put one in the barn too. Also, we wondered if you had come up with any numbers to call. If so, we can get on that. I'm sure they would want to know that you are okay, especially that boss of yours."

"Okay, I feel better knowing we have a plan. I made a list of numbers and names. I really think whoever calls should use a public phone."

"All right, good idea." and he gave her a big hug. "I miss having you up at the house. You'll be back up there again soon."

Chapter 23

Riley was restless. Working from home had its benefits, but it could get boring quick if the house was too quiet. Jack was at work and not allowed to come home until the end of their day. She hoped they found the director soon. Everyone was worried about him and Mary. She especially missed Mary and her calls to just talk. Being struck in this house, she waited for word about either of them.

The phone rang, and she thought, another telemarketer, oh great. she answered, even though she thought to just let it ring.

"Hello."

"Hello, Riley?"

"Mary?!"

"I'm here with my uncle and his family. I wanted to let the people at Benton center know I'm safe, but there are some bad men after the director and me. He decided to let them take him so he could find out what they wanted. I'm sure they have him by now. Can you let Jack know so he can tell everyone? Tell him to do it face to face, don't call or text anyone, they might track your cellphones. I'll call again, if I can. Stay safe." and the phone went dead.

Riley sat in stunned silence. Her first impulse was to call Jack, but Mary had said the bad guys might trace the cellphone. She looked at the clock. Two hours, he would be home in two hours. She sat and worried. It was the longest two hours of her life.

Two hours later, Jack walked in the door. He was surprised to find Riley almost bouncing at the door. "What's going on?" he asked.

"You will not believe! Mary's safe on her uncle's farm. Jack, she told me to tell you face to face, and that you should tell everyone at work in person. The people who are after them might trace any calls we get on our cellphones."

"That's great news about Mary. What about the director?" Jack asked as he gave her a hug. Riley explained about the director. "At least, we know that Mary's safe."

After sharing that news, the rest of the evening was more upbeat. Jack looked forward to sharing his news at work, and Riley was so happy about good news about Mary, they broke out a bottle of wine to celebrate after so many days of worry. At bedtime, they found they wanted to hold each other tight in happiness.

Jack got to work early the next day. He was happy about Mary, but he still was apprehensive about the director. Nobody had seen or heard from him for days. Ahead of him, he saw Alex, the signal processing manager. He hurried to catch up.

"Alex, can I have a few words privately?"

"Privately? I don't know where that would be in this facility. Let me try to find a place where we can talk," and he walked away.

Jack turned into the pit to go to his seat. The pit was the semi-circle of positions of various instrumentation used to study space. Some gathered the signals, some did diagnostics, and some did analysis. Jack sighed because it was very boring to sit in front of his screen and not be able to do his job. He looked around the area and noticed that some people were staring at their screens, some were reading, and some were sleeping at their stations. He wondered what the mood would be when they learn that, at least, Mary was safe.

Jack kept an eye out for Alex, but he didn't see him anywhere. As he left for a restroom break, he took a detour up the stairs toward Alex's office. Before he arrived, however, he heard voices coming from the office. They were getting louder. He kept moving closer, but he moved slower too, as he started to understand what was being said.

"I have done everything you have asked. It's not my fault you can't get anything out of the Director! He didn't tell me if he was planning on seeing anyone else except someone at ISMC. Now you tell me it was the Director of ISMC, Dr. Harold Cummings. I didn't know he was going to the top man. Talk to him! What do you mean, both of them have disappeared? You better get them back before the entire plan falls through."

Jack heard the phone slam down and knew he better get back to his desk. He hurried back to the restroom. After standing in a stall for a minute, he headed back to his desk. Alex was looking around while he stood behind Jack's chair.

"Let's go up to my office and talk," Alex said.

"Sure," Jack agreed, and followed Alex.

"This office should be safe to talk. What did you want to tell me?"

Jack stammered that it was sensitive and he babbled the first excuse that came to him. He hoped Riley would forgive him for using her in his excuse to Alex, but after overhearing what Alex had said on his phone call, he would not tell him about Mary.

"I have a problem. I need time off to take Riley to the doctor. She has a bad injury in her right foot. It's bad enough that she can't put any pressure on it, which means she can't drive. I know we are on lockdown and no one is allowed off, but she needs me now."

"I don't know if I can get you that time. I sympathize with her pain; I've been there too. I'll ask. It's the only thing I can promise. Okay?"

"Can I ask about how long it will take to get an answer?"

"Oh, I think you'll know by tomorrow. Thanks for coming to me and I hope Riley feels better soon," Alex offered in reply, he needed to mobilize a unit to double-check Jack's story.

"Thank you and sorry I had to bother you."

Jack headed straight back to his station. He wondered how Riley will feel about faking a painful foot. He thought about his very active wife and wondered if she could slow down enough.

Jack caught Alex watching him throughout the day. He hoped he hadn't been too clever with his answer.

Later, he jumped in his seat when suddenly Alex spoke from directly behind his chair.

"I bet Riley is going crazy being immobile with a bad foot. I can't imagine it."

"Sorry you caught me zoned out. You are right about Riley, she's not a good patient. She always has a lot of energy and this is hard on her. I really want to get her to the doctor so she feels better."

"Do you know what's wrong? Did she sprain it or something?"

"I don't know. She said she was doing several things at the same time and slipped on a stair."

"So, you didn't see the accident yourself."

"No, I had just got here when it happened. She thought nothing about it at first, but the longer she waits, the worst the pain gets. She really should see a doctor or at least get to urgent care. Have you heard about my time off?"

"Yes, you can take tomorrow off, no problem, especially since it's Friday. I hope you can get in to see a doctor. I hope Riley feels better soon."

"Thanks, Alex, I really appreciate you going to bat for us."

"Good luck, buddy," Alex said as he gave Jack a pat on his back.

Jack was so happy when the day ended. His shoulders hurt because he had been under stress all day thinking about what he had heard., and he wanted to get home to warn Riley. He had wanted to call her and talk with her about all this, but he didn't feel it was safe for either of them. They couldn't take the chance of someone listening in on their conversation.

There was a strange truck in the driveway when he got home. He hurried into the house to find Riley on the couch talking to a man about television service.

"Oh good, you are on the couch. You know you are not to be on your foot." To cover Riley's look of surprise, he turned to the man.

"Saw your truck in the driveway, I'm Jack, Riley's husband. And you are?" he asked as he held out his hand. The man's attention immediately switched to Jack.

"Sorry for taking your space in the driveway. I'm Stan and I work for Central TV Service. We're new in the area and I was introducing myself to people in the neighborhood."

"Honey, are you unhappy with our present service? She is the one who decides the TV service."

"Well, I explained that we really were happy with our service, but I would listen to what the new service might offer."

"I was just telling her about our expanded satellite coverage that will increase the number of programs being offered and other unique programming. All for a modest price of $55 per month, plus you can purchase additional services, like a deluxe remote, for a small additional charge."

"I have the brochure with all the information, but I think we'll keep our present service. We appreciate you stopping by and letting us know of the new option," Riley told the salesman.

"Stay on the couch, I'll see Stan out," said Jack as he moved to the door.

Holding his finger to his lips to mean silence, he asked her, "hope your foot is feeling better. I got tomorrow off to take you to a doctor. I hope we can get an appointment, but if we can't I'll take you to urgent care."

"Thank you dear, you always take good care of me."

"Always," he said as he gave her a kiss. He whispered in her ear, "was he here very long? Did he stay in this room?"

At her nod, he started going through the room for bugs. He ran his hands over and under all the furniture. He finally found one on the underside of the marble top of the side table. When Riley saw the bug, she reacted with anger. While she seethed on the couch, he got out some paper and pens and wrote a note.

"I imagine you are tired of being on the couch, but knowing you, I bet you were on your foot longer than you should have been. Why don't we go into the dining room and have some tea, then I'll make dinner? Here let me help you." He told her as he continued to look for bugs.

He wrote, "Act natural. I'll explain later. Important."

She nodded her understanding and said, "let's have the new box of tea, I think its green tea and I have some biscotti."

"Sounds good to me." He took the bug and put it in the trash. "I'll clean the house for you so you can relax. I don't think we can get in to see your doctor, so I can take you to urgent care tomorrow. Maybe I can get you a cane?" he teased her. She retaliated by hitting his shoulder with her pillow.

Later, he ran the sweeper and put all trash together in one big bag. Then he took it out to the large dumpster down the street from their house. He and Riley spent the rest of the evening in the quiet of their bedroom discussing everything that had happened that day. Finally, they fell into an exhausted sleep, hoping the next day would be better.

Chapter 24

Riley and Jack talked about how they could spread the news about Mary's safety and the conversation Jack had overheard. He couldn't think of a way to do it at work, so it fell to Riley to find a way. She didn't have to playact being bored when she had to wear the boot on her foot or use a cane. In the house it wasn't so bad, but if they went anywhere, she had to use them. The hardest thing was she couldn't drive with it, so she had to stay home. Today, she would put into action an idea they had come up with the night before.

"Hi Cora. I haven't been out of my house for a couple of days and I'm going crazy. Ha ha, I know I have always been crazy, but I was wondering if you would want to get together tomorrow. I will call Arabella and Sandi to see if they also want to come too. We can play cards or just talk. Maybe we could make two card tables and invite Juan and the baby and maybe Raj too."

"Riley, I'm sure the two guys could use a break too. That sounds great. I'm in and I'll bring sandwiches to share. What time?"

"How about 12:30 on Monday? That way everyone can get home in time for the kids to get out of school."

"Great, see you then."

Riley made calls to the others, and they were all coming over and bringing something to share. Cleaning the house and picking a dessert to make from what she had on hand took a while. Jack had done the shopping, and she thought he went a little overboard. She supplied him with a list, but he added things that caught his eye. Drinks were easy because they now had a selection of four or five different brands of soda, and numerous coffees and teas. It took two hours to pull out tablecloths, playing cards, and pretty plates and tableware. Seeing Juan and Marcella's new four-month-old baby will be wonderful. *That baby was just so cute*, she thought as she prepared an area for her to play. Juan was really enjoying being a stay-at-home dad. He loved being able to work from home which was really handy and Marcella loved her job at Benton. Riley was really getting excited to have her friends over for a good time, even though she had an important mission to do with this get together.

She greeted everyone at exactly 12:30, laughing at Cora who wore a hot pink bow in her hair. Cora blushed and explained that her daughter insisted that she wear it all day because her momma needed something cheerful today. All the friends agreed that the little one had the right idea.

Amid a lot of laughter and joking about how Riley hurt her foot, she led her guests to the dining room to eat some lunch. They shared recipes, pictures of their kids and even some of their achievements and everyone played with the baby. Riley and Jack had only been married a short time, but she was ready to add to her little family someday soon, so she listened eagerly to all the stories and daydreamed. She even shared a dream she'd had about her ideal family where she and Jack had three daughters. They always wore white dresses and never got dirty. Her friends choked over that detail.

"Just wait," laughed Cora.

"I have a request first. Can I have all your phones? Here, just put them in the basket. We don't want any interruptions while we play," Riley said as she passed around a basket.

"Oh, okay. As long as you promise to return it," Raj said, laughing.

"I promise to return them," she said as she walked into the kitchen where she placed the basket in the refrigerator.

After lunch, they moved to the tables to play cards. After a while, Riley casually mentioned Mary's name. Everyone expressed dismay that no one knew where she was.

"Well, I kind of have some news about her. I had a phone call from her. Mary is safe and staying with her uncle and family."

"What do you mean safe? She left with the director. Surely, she's safe with him," Sandi questioned her.

"Well, the phone call also came with a warning to only talk face to face because of bugs on our phones or in our houses. Jack and I had a man visit who said his name was Stan, and that he was from a new TV service company in the area. After he left, Jack searched the living room and found a bug."

Everyone started talking at the same time. Riley waited until it died down and then laid everything out for them. They listened to her story about what Jack had heard, the phone call from Mary, and the man who had come to their house, and lastly, the fake injury to her foot.

"What can we do to protect ourselves and our families?" Arabella, whose husband also worked at Benton, asked.

"Yes, there are definitely things we all can do. A lot of our husbands, wives or friends work at Benton. One is to not use our phones to talk about any of this, because they could bug or track any of our phones. We thought to first, buy a burner phone so we can communicate with each other, and second is to tell everyone face to face about Mary being safe so they can tell the other people at work, but only face to face. Even more disturbing is what Jack overheard when Alex was talking on the phone. The only thing we could think to do is to not talk to him about anything personal."

"Okay, my family can do that," said Cora. All chorused her agreement.

"I think we should get together regularly, say once a week for lunch or dinner or more often if events warrant it. That way we can talk and keep up on any recent developments," supplied Sandi. Everyone agreed with that.

Raj looked at his watch. "Oops, I got to go. It's a little later than I thought." All of them looked surprised at the time and quickly gathered their things. Riley hurried to retrieve the cellphones from the refrigerator.

Everyone bade Riley goodbye and hurried out to their cars. Riley felt a lot better about everything, and now she felt that she and Jack were not all alone dealing with this mess.

Chapter 25

Dan got home to his wife, and Malinda got home to her cat without incident. Malinda nervously reported to work the next day. They were unsure what might be waiting for them. They expected strange men in black to be waiting at their doors, but no one was there.

"Malinda, no one strange has shown up at my office, no one stranger than me."

"Dan, you always make me laugh. You are right, no one has shown up at my door either. I hope it continues like that."

"Well, call if you hear voices. I could use a laugh."

"Okay, will do," Malinda answered as she turned to take some rock samples to her lab. She barely got through the door of her lab before a hand holding a soaked cloth closed over her mouth. It only took two breaths and she was out. The stranger laid her down on the floor of her lab and tied her hands and taped her mouth so she couldn't alert anyone while he got her over to Dan's office. He had a laundry cart ready, and he put her in it and covered her with a white sheet, then he and the cart left to visit Dan in another building.

An article in a prestigious magazine engrossed Dan. He was so interested in it; he didn't hear his door open until it was too late. He regained consciousness to find Malinda lying beside him on the floor of his office. Her hands and feet were tied and her mouth was taped.

"Oh, no, Malinda, can you hear me? Please wake up." He tried to watch to see if she was breathing okay. Malinda groaned. "That's good, wake up now."

Malinda groggily shook her head and she opened her eyes and looked around. Dan could see her trying to push the tape off her mouth.

"I think those men have caught up with us," he said calmly as he laid on the floor with his hands tied behind his back.

She nodded her agreement as she continued to try to loosen the tape.

"I think he's still here, but I don't know where," he whispered.

Suddenly, a man dressed all in black stepped into view. He quickly stepped to Dan and taped his mouth shut too. Then he began to drag him over to a larger cart where he starting to lift Dan up to place him in the cart. He didn't see the man and woman who had just stepped into Dan's office. Startled, he dropped Dan. At the same moment, the two new visitors did two things. One, the man yelled, "Hey, what are you doing?!" and two, the woman screamed and fainted and fell backward into the hall. At the sound of people running toward the office, the man dressed in black took off running out of the office, down the hall knocking over everything in his way, and then down the nearest stairwell.

It wasn't too long before the noise drew even more notice. It stunned them to see the distinguished doctor tied up and lying on the floor, and they recognized Malinda as a frequent visitor of the Doctor's.

"Quick, call campus security, will you? Maybe they can catch the man who did this." They described how the man was dressed all in black. "Hurry, hurry," he said after someone took the tape off his mouth and as co-workers worked to untie their hands. "He's probably driving a black SUV," he added.

Campus security rushed into the room in time to hear the description Dan rattled off. The officer radioed the description out to other officers and it was not long when they heard that they had the man and were bringing him to the office so Dan and Malinda could identify him. While they waited, Dan and Malinda sat down and drink water that their co-workers brought them and Dan had his head wound looked at by his friend. Soon, they heard footsteps.

Security came in holding a man dressed all in black between them. "We found him getting into a black SUV. Is he your attacker?"

Malinda looked him over and grasped when she saw he was clutching something in his hand. She grabbed his hand and plied it open and out fell a brooch. "Why would you take my brooch?" She bent to pick it up, and the man took advantage of everyone's attention being on her and the brooch to break away from the men holding him. Suddenly, he went still and screamed. He just faded away.

"Where did he go?" Malinda dropped her brooch in amazement. Pandemonium reined as everyone started talking at the same time. Dan's colleague fainted again. Luckily, a security guard caught her as she collapsed.

"Well, that was exciting," Dan said in his most droll voice.

Chapter 26

Neither Harold nor Henry slept well in their new home. Being in their hiding place still didn't manage to ease their minds that they were safe. Plus, the additional uncertainty for his team weighed heavily on the director. The last time he had seen them, they had all been excited about the signal and re-energized in their jobs. A new vitality had seemed to enter the hub. He and Mary had started this trip hoping to get an answer to their question. It had gone downhill quickly, and the director wondered what he could have done differently, or who else they could have called for help.

Well, what's done is done. Now we just have to get out of this muddle, he thought. *And Mary, I hope she made it okay and is truly safe.*

Harold and Henry seemed to have the same idea at the same time. They both rolled out of their bunks.

"Need some coffee?" they both asked at the same time. "Director, we have a visitor." They both looked up at the speaker at the same time. Harold smiled and said, "I think he is informing me that the men in black have found us."

"On our way," Harold said to the speaker. "Come on," he said to Henry.

Both hurried to the viewing hub in the bunker to determine who their visitor was. The officers had calibrated the equipment to not pay attention to anything smaller than a house cat. They both hoped it was a false alarm, or was just someone wandering by.

"Who is it? Can you identify how many there are?" Harold asked his technician.

"We're looking at six heat signatures, sir. It looks like a recon detail."

"Are we still camouflaged from the outside? Or do we need to break out the cool suits?" Harold inquired.

"Sir, I would get the cool suits, just in case. We don't know what their firepower is yet. They seem too interested in this building."

Harold hurried to a cabinet and took enough cool suits for everybody in the room. He didn't worry too much for the people sleeping downstairs. They vented those rooms with outside air and then cooled them so the everyone would get better rest. Their body temperatures should already be low enough.

"Good thing, sir, here comes the heat signature gun."

Everyone held their breath as the man dressed in black read the heat signatures of everyone in the building, except the body temperatures of the men downstairs in the protected basement bedrooms. Then one man rose up and pointed a shoulder-fired rocket launcher at the front of the building.

"Now we will find out if our defenses hold," said Harold into the tense silence.

The people inside the room felt the explosion, but when the smoke cleared, they saw that the "brick" held. It looked a little dented but was still solid. A sigh went up from the room. It was good to know that the technology of seventy years ago was still good. That was because it wasn't actually brick, but a composite material made to resist a nuclear blast. They watched as the man outside reloaded the rocket launcher. Harold turned and stepped back to the cabinets and started handing out the various guns and ammunition it held.

Henry roused the sleeping people and bought them up to date on recent developments. They immediately prepared themselves and snatched what they could to eat and drink. They provided food and drink to the men and women in the hub as they waited. No one knew how long the defenses would last, but one hope was that one rocket launcher would limit the damage done. They had faith in the construction, but it had never been tested outside of the lab.

The technician continued to monitor the number of combatants arrayed outside. The number remained at six, with one man holding the rocket launcher and another man handing ammunition up to him.

"Is there any way we can get one of our people outside to take out that launcher?" wondered Henry. "Or maybe a two-person team?"

"I don't know. Brian, where is the map of this facility?"

"Yes, sir. Just a moment." He ran to a cabinet and riffled through a set of rolled blueprints. He snatched one and then ran back to spread it open on a table. Harold and Henry gathered around it with Brian. Brian traced the entrances and Henry traced the tunnels where the ducts were located.

"What about these?" asked Henry, tapping his finger on one tunnel that seemed to have a door to the outside in the rear of the building.

Harold studied the blueprint and asked for two volunteers to explore the tunnel and, if possible, gain outside access. It looked like, if they could get the door open, it would gain them a route around the side of the building. They might pull off a surprise assault on the six men seeking to get through the front.

"I need a two-volunteers to explore this tunnel, and see if it allows outside access, seek to find a path around the building to take these people out. I need two more to give them cover," said Harold.

Although Brian's hand went up, Harold stopped him. "Not you, son. I need you right here to monitor the teams. I need to know what's going on. Sorry."

Harold and Henry remained behind the technician with their eyes glued to the screen. They saw four white dots moving down the tunnel. "Sorry, sir. There are no live feeds in the tunnel system. We only get these blips showing movement. Once they are outside, we'll get a live feed. They have microphones on, so you can talk to them."

"That's good. We'll use what we have."

Very tense minutes went by before they signaled that they were at the outside door. The technician scanned all the outside feeds to see where the combatants stood. He counted them and all six were in front of the building. He signaled Harold and then gave the men in the tunnel the okay to open the door and head out.

Harold and Henry shifted to the monitor with a live feed. There they watched the first team head out and around the first corner of the building. As the team traveled around the perimeter, they changed monitors to keep them in sight. Soon, they were joined by the second team. Finally, the team was in position, and with one sighted on the rocket launcher and the other sighted on the other men arrayed around him. The covering team took position to cover the remaining enemy combatants. There was the sound of a snap and the rocket launcher blew up in the man's hands leaving his hands bloody, but otherwise he was unharmed. The stunned men froze, and the other attacking men quickly fired at the door they had been trying to pierce, not noticing the two teams ease back around the corner and back to the tunnel door.

"Now, that was damn fine shooting," one technician yelled and then blushed in embarrassment.

"That's okay, it was damn fine shooting," Henry affirmed, grinning at the soldier. "I'm glad we didn't kill anyone. After all, we still don't know who they are or why they were so interested in us."

As the two teams came back into the hub, the technician called to Harold and the director. "Sir, something is developing outside. It doesn't make any sense."

Everyone went to the monitor and stared at the figures standing motionless outside. They looked puzzled, and then they were just gone. Disappeared. On the ground where they had stood were their guns, including the remains of the rocket launcher. The man who had held the launcher had disappeared, but he had left behind some blood pooling on the ground.

"Can you widen the radius of our scans? Can we see if there are any more attackers out there?" Harold asked the technician.

"I'll try, sir, but the scanner was already near maximum radius."

"Let's send some people out there to make sure they are gone and bring back those weapons," Harold ordered. "Be very careful."

The small group moved out and searched the entire area only to find the weapons on the ground and a small pool of blood. They returned to the building with the retrieved items and a sample of the blood, but as they entered the hub the sample of blood also disappeared.

"Just do what you can to clean the area." Harold told the confused technician. He turned to everyone there. "Good job, thanks to all."

Henry turned to Harold and said, "I only wish we knew what they wanted."

Chapter 27

Mary had read all the data that the director had packed for the trip to the ISMC Atlanta office. She didn't see what information the men in black could need so badly that they would go to such lengths to achieve. She was suffering from boredom, so she headed up to the main floor of the barn to see her favorite animal, her horse. There had been no sign of the intruders for the last few days. She thought she heard noises, so she grabbed her gun and climbed up to say hello to her uncle or cousin.

When she went up the steps, she noticed that the horses were very nervous and agitated. Her first impulse was to move to them, but she remained where she was and listened and examined her surroundings first. She didn't move to them, but she sensed nothing that could cause their nervousness. Still, she waited.

The first sign of real trouble was the shying of the horses to the farthest corner of their stalls where they started kicking the boards. Still, she continued to wait, not moving at all. A shadow slid down the wall. She moved her eyes to follow it. She quickly calculated where the individual was in the barn. Whoever it was, they were slowly descending from the rafters.

She slowly lifted her gun and sighted along the line and fired. The result was very gratifying as the person screamed as they dropped. Immediately, she dropped back down the steps and slammed the cover down and locked it. She took a covered positioned where she could shoot along a line of sight to the stairs, there she grabbed her phone and quickly made a call to her uncle and cousin who were working out in the fields. They were probably too far away to help, but could get here to protect her aunt.

She heard many footfalls over her head. It was too many to be her relatives, so she arranged her weapons around her so they were within reach. The opening to her hiding place slowly swung up out of sight. Her throwing knives went first and thudded into calves and feet as the men tried to come down the stairs. She grabbed her slingshot as the men backed off. Today, finally all of her childhood practice with Davy trying to strike targets that Nick had hung up on various trees of varied distances would pay off. She had lined up her ammunition of small stones, after that she had large throwing rocks, and then the last resort of her gun.

Suddenly, they charged down the steps two at a time. She kept busy firing off the small projectiles which all hit someone because they were so cramped on the steps. The stones were striking and ricocheting from man to man causing confusion and painful injuries. She used larger stones when she ran out of small stones which created additional discord among her attackers. Then she reached for her gun.

"Stay down, you bastards," she yelled at them as they tried to get up. Startled, they hesitated. She fired at their feet and threatened, "stay down or the next bullet will take you down."

A man's voice screamed at them, "take her now!" They looked conflicted, but they were clearly more scared of him than her. They rushed her, and she fired, hitting a few. Suddenly they stiffened and simply faded away.

She stared at where they had been. Blood still smeared the floor and steps. Their guns, knives, and other objects littered the floor. They were just gone. Slowly, she mounted the steps up to the main floor of the barn. The agitated horses were no longer kicking their stalls to get out. She moved to soothe them as she looked around the barn at the weapons lying on the floor.

Amy came running in, carrying her rifle. She stared at Mary and the weapons and blood on the floor.

"I guess you'll tell me about what happened here."

"Yeah, as soon as I figure it out for myself. All I know is one moment they were attacking and then they were just gone, poof!"

"Well, Nick and Davy will be here soon. Gunshots travel a long way over farmland."

"Look, the blood has disappeared too," Mary cried.

"What in the world is going on?" Amy said in wonderment.

Chapter 28

Jack got to work a little early and immediately sensed something wasn't right. Some systems were completely dead and others were giving weird readings. Since the employees had not touched their stations for days, the stations should have been dark, but they weren't.

"What's happening?" he asked several people. They just shook their heads and said they didn't know.

Others in the hub were searching under desks, or writing down which stations were acting up and which stations were dead.

The person everyone knew as Alex was standing at the railing overlooking the hub, laughing. It was then that everything clicked for Jack.

"What did you do?" Jack yelled up at him. Several people looked up in surprise.

Alex turned his head and seemed to see him for the first time. Smiling, he stood calmly and continued to watch the chaos.

"It's beautiful, isn't it? All the smoke and fire, all the beautiful mess, and all because of one signal from outer space. All those other signals were nothing. Ahh, but that one signal changed everything. Your beloved director, gone, your so-called great machines, gone. You will never know where that signal came from or where it was going. You are all just stupid pigs being ruled. Ruled is what you need, and you need us! We are your masters now." He had spoken softly, like he was speaking to a child, but the more he spoke the louder he got till he finished his lecture at a near scream.

"What did you do?" Jack demanded again as more and more co-workers arrived. They stared in disbelief at the destruction around them as they listened to the words.

A few of them ran for the fire extinguishers and began battling the fires around the room. A few made moves to confront Alex.

"That won't do you any good, you know. I rigged it so nothing in this room will ever work again. And the beauty of it is you don't know what I did, except the fires of course. I so like a good fire. It will be wonderful. I wish I could stay to watch, but I have to leave now," Alex said as he reached down and picked up a grenade. "It was such fun while it lasted." He made a move to remove the pin, but suddenly he screamed "NO, not now," and dropped the grenade and grabbed his head. Then he just faded away.

"What the hell was that?" someone said.

Others ran to secure the grenade and others stood gawking at where Alex had been a few moments ago.

Jack brought them back to practicalities. "Pedro, can you get those fires under control? Mike, did you get the grenade?

Let's look for anything out of place. Thanks people, glad we are all still here." They gave him an uncertain wave or smile in reply.

At first, they just stared at him as if he had lost his mind, but his reasonable words sunk in and they moved to do as instructed.

He moved up to the spot where Alex had faded out and noted the various items left behind. He nodded to the men there, but didn't stop. He moved on up to Alex's office and looked there for any note or scrap of evidence of who or what Alex had been. He found a note that talked about the director and Mary, but it seemed to be in another language. The languages he had studied in high school and college were romance languages, like French, Italian, and Spanish. He remembered Marcella was fluent in the Baltic languages. Maybe he could read it.

"Marcella, can you come up here?" he called down into the hub. A few minutes later, Marcella came into the room.

"Can you read this?" he asked hopefully. "It isn't one of the Romance languages."

"And I'm sorry, it isn't the language in the Baltic either. Have you tried Russian? I think Aaron speaks Russian or one of the Slavic languages. It really doesn't look like it's Chinese or Hindu. It also doesn't look like Arabic."

"Thanks, can you locate Aaron and send him up here?" Jack asked her.

"Sure, sorry, I couldn't help. Don't feel too bad, there are over two hundred languages."

Both of them stared in astonishment as the note also faded away. "Darn it, now we don't have any evidence," Jack said exasperated.

Chapter 29

"Pebble?" a voice spoke to it, but no one was there. It scanned its surroundings and didn't see anyone. The family had moved back into their home when the men in black had not returned. Again, the voice came, but this time it registered that it came from inside of it. Pebble became very still. This differed from anything it had felt before.

"Pebble, it's okay. I will send my image through the drone so you can see me." Pebble was puzzled. The voice spoke in a language it hadn't heard in a very long time.

"Pebble? Are you okay?" Jenny's sleepy voice came from nearby. He heard footsteps and knew Jenny was moving to get him.

It called out for Tom and Colleen. Tom woke up and Colleen stirred when he moved. Together they moved into Jenny's bedroom to find her already up and searching for Pebble in the dark. Tom turned on a small lamp. "What's wrong, sweet?" he asked as Jenny grabbed Pebble and held it close.

"Jenny, my people come," Pebble told Jenny.

"What? Now?" Tom said as he looked everywhere in the bedroom, imagining the small room covered in little pebbles. Colleen took his hand, and they both calmed down.

"He comes now," Pebble cried out to the family.

Suddenly a figure materialized in front of them. The figure was striking in appearance, with strong features, including large silver eyes that radiated friendliness and kindness. He was tall, much taller than Tom, but he stood entirely at ease in a metallic looking blue suit. He spoke, but the only sound was a run of unintelligent syllables. He paused and shook his head. Then he stepped forward and put his hands on either side of Tom's head and as Tom stiffened the figure laid his forehead gently on Tom's forehead. They stood together for a few moments with Colleen, Jenny and Pebble watching them.

"Don't be alarmed, Tom. I need to access the language in your mind and copy it to my mind so I can talk with you. It won't harm you, but it is draining on your energy," Zebut calmly told him mentally.

When the figure stepped back, Tom blinked and crumpled. Colleen and Jenny jumped to Tom's side. Colleen confronted the stranger, "if you have harmed him, I'll…"

A deep voice said, "he will be all right in a moment. I needed the language to communicate with you. Sorry to have alarmed you."

"I'm okay," Tom said and took Colleen's hand. "Who are you?"

"My name is Zebut. I am a descendant of the people who originally sent Pebble out into space to find a home for us. This little drone had an amazing trip to this world and an amazing journey since it had arrived. We thank you for freeing it from the geode, and we honor it and you." Zebut bowed deeply to all of them. "We sent millions of small drones out in a desperate plan to save as much of our world as we could. We gave the drones artificial intelligence to allow them to make decisions, and we gave them the power to send messages to us if they found an unoccupied world. Pebble is special and unique; as we did not give them the means to generate replacements of themselves."

"Are you here on Earth? How are we seeing and hearing you?" Colleen asked.

"No, I wish I could be there in person, but I am on my planet. The first Maven was our planet of origin, but our sun went nova and we had to leave. Maven was chosen as the name of our new home world in honor to that original world. Pebble was one of millions of drones we sent out to look for a new home. It amazed us to learn of Pebble and its long journey. The drone that answered Pebble's reports forwarded us details on what was taking place here. Tottahagan is the planet of these troublemakers, and they cause problems throughout this part of the galaxy, so I am here to repair what damage they have caused."

"You can do that?" Tom said in wonderment.

"We are an advanced race, considered advanced long before our sun went nova many thousands of years ago, and now we continue to learn a lot about our new region of space. Over time, we have joined a Council of Planets and have become the overseers of peace in our region."

"We didn't know who the men in black really were. They could have been foreign agents of an unfriendly government or from our own government. We named them 'men in black' because of the way they dressed and after a movie by that name. I'm afraid our world is pretty messed up," Tom told him. "You probably never had the problems we have."

"There you would be wrong. My people also went through a period of revolution when we were young. We were lucky because we survived long enough to gain wisdom. Almost all intelligent life goes through the same stage of growth. Our sun forced us to band together to survive. It took us a very long time to send our people out into the unknown and to send our seekers to find a new home. In that time, we learned to respect and trust each other."

"What will happen to these men? Do they have a name?"

"They come from the planet far from here, called Tottaha-gan. We have discovered them spread across your planet, and they are being transported from your planet right now while we talk. I need to seek your permission if my superiors say we need your help, can we come back? My apologies, my time with you grows short." He turned to Pebble. "I need to ask you an important question. Do you wish to stay here? If you stay, you will not see us again and we do not plan to contact you again except in a dire emergency. Take a little time to think about this. Let me know when you have your answer."

Pebble looked at each member of the family, finally looking at Jenny. "I wish to stay with Jenny."

"Wait, can't we still continue contact with you and your people?" Tom questioned in dismay. He had so many questions.

"Your planet is still developing in wisdom. That is something that takes many generations. We will return if we need your help bringing Tottahagan to justice, other than that we would not contact you until we find you have developed enough in wisdom to join us or if we need your help. Space is full of unknown perils and you are not ready yet. Goodbye friends. Now we will think of you and will be protecting you. But we won't intrude in your decisions," he said as he slowly faded from sight.

Chapter 30

They had the agents from Tottahagan in group cells on Maven. Each group got the same indifferent treatment. Each cell had a floor that formed the beds and other furniture, but would not form other items that might be a weapon. The worried, bored and surly prisoners wanted to smash something, anything, and the only thing in the rooms was the ever-accommodating floor. If they broke their bed, it flowed back into the floor. The only thing that was different was that the floor did not produce another bed. The room then had one less bed in it. After a while, the prisoners realized that if they broke all the furniture, soon some rooms would have no furniture in them at all and they would have to sit or sleep on the ground.

The guards patrolling the prisoners were soon laughing as they saw some cells completely without furniture, others with a bed for everyone to sit on, or some with just a table.

Zebut watched them thoughtfully, noting those rooms where some prisoners would quarrel and one would try to use reason. Other cells contained, it seemed, no one with any thought or sense about what they were losing by destruction.

Zebut watched and learned a lot by watching, not just the prisoners, but also the guards as they carefully manipulated the cells. First, in every cell, they would have the floor form a desk with a paper on it that said, "I confess…"

At first, Zebut saw the prisoners ignore it, but sometimes it remained available for a while before it again flowed into the floor. Zebut asked the guards to softly play into the cells the most recent recorded message from one of the prisoners to Tottahagan. He hoped that they might wonder what was being said or know the voices. The guards agreed, and the results did not take long in developing.

"You, you're responsible for us failing our mission," yelled one tall, dark-haired man in a cell of six. It confused Zebut to see the man disappear as he launched himself across the cell. Then he looked up and saw the man materialize in a cell across from him. The angry man was now by himself in a cell that had all its furniture where he sat glaring at a man with blond hair who was slumped against a wall alone in the cell across from him. Again, the desk appeared in all the cells, again with a paper on it that read, "I confess to the following crimes against the planet Earth…" A few men signed the paper and they instantly disappeared and did not appear in any of the surrounding cells. That got the men murmuring among themselves. Again, the message played softly in the background and more of the men listened. Again, they looked at the man in the cell across from them.

One man in a cell with six men was sitting on the floor, leaning against the wall, saying again and again, "It's not fair, it's not fair." He continued the mantra as he eyed the solitary man slumped in the cell across the hall. His fellow cellmates also eyed him warily. Suddenly, he spoke louder and louder, and he shoved up from the floor. This caused his fellow prisoners to get to their feet. As the man propelled himself toward the boundary of their cell, his fellow prisoners grabbed him and pressed him back against the wall. They talked and talked until the man seemed to take notice to what they were saying. Slowly, he nodded and slid back down to sit on the floor. One man remained with him, listening to him and responding. Suddenly, the floor flowed into benches for the prisoners in that cell. The sight started a lot of debate.

Again, the message played, this time a little louder in all the cells. Again, the floor flowed into a desk with the paper on it that said. "I confess to the following crimes..." As more men got up and signed the paper, they too disappeared. The remaining men looked at each other and started talking.

Zebut watched it all and marveled at the beauty of it. He switched views to the men who had signed the confession. Each man had two guards talking to them about what their confessions meant. After that, they took them to their cells, where the doors were open to a common area so they could mingle and socialize. An assigned task gave each man something to do every day, such as laundry or cooking. It didn't surprise Zebut when the men seemed relieved to have something to do with their time. It was a good sign. Maybe they will find it more rewarding to have honest work than taking risks for someone who didn't care about them. Watching them gave him the beginnings of an idea for a plan of action to submit to the Tottahagan leadership for the future lives of these men.

Zebut returned his attention to the lone man in his cell. He needed to reach him somehow, to show him that there was another way. He asked the psychologist on duty.

"Dr. Douro, thank you for meeting with me," Zebut said as he bowed.

"How can I help you?" The doctor asked as he bowed back to Zebut.

"There is a patient here as a detainee. He is from Tottahagan and has carried out several crimes against another planet. He will return to his home world soon, but I want to submit a plan of treatment to the experts on his home world. He came here with numerous fellow prisoners, but evidence points to him being a possible leader. Can you do a series of evaluations on him to diagnose why he acts as he does?"

"Yes, we have several tests that we can run that will help narrow down his motivations. We also can examine him to ensure that he is physically healthy, such as no blockages or hemorrhages. I can get those done as soon as possible."

"I appreciate your efforts in this matter."

Zebut went back to his office to start on his report and to write a plan of action for the prisoners, and he found they had also delivered the first report of tests on the prisoners. He wanted to take something concrete to Tottahagan that they could really use. He started with his report, which detailed the crimes committed and the names of those who committed them. He also wanted to include the confession each man submitted.

This was his first major test as a prosecutor, and he wanted to be very thorough. A soft chime sounded and he looked up to see the confessions and accompanying scans of most of the prisoners come in on his computer. He noticed that the only one missing was the information from the psychologist on the possible leader. That report, he was sure, would take longer.

Some hours later he was surprised at how quickly they sent the report on that last man to his desk computer. The doctor gave a diagnosis of borderline personality disorder. He proposed that the prisoner receive supervised meetings with a psychologist because of his severe mood swings and poor self-image. These meetings could help the man learn better coping strategies for his conditions. Otherwise, the man was physically healthy.

Zebut finished his report and sent a copy to his mother for her critique. He was ready. He was nervous, but also satisfied that he had done his best.

Chapter 31

The next day Zebut found he was more than a little nervous. He had assembled all the evidence, and prepared his deposition and now he needed to get the final okay from the Council. Again, he travelled down to his mother's office. He laid out the evidence collected and his detailed plan of action for the officials on Tottahagan. He ended with his plan of action for the prisoners and a written application for an audience with the Council. He almost wished he had the brave little drone here with him. The thought made him smile.

"Relax Zebut, you have done an outstanding job. It either will work or it won't. You know two councilors must accompany the prime negotiator according to procedure, I will be one of them and the council will determine the other. You know what to do after that. Be strong, be persuasive. Come, the council is waiting."

Zebut was nervous, but his mother quickly gave his hand a squeeze.

After entering the High Chamber of the Council, Zebut mounted the podium as the Prosecutor of the case and bowed deeply to the seated councilors. He remained in that position until they called his name.

"Tor-Kon Zebut, you stand as the prosecutor for the case against the government of Tottahagan. These are high crimes against another planet, called Earth. Planet Earth does not have their own representation because of their early stage of development. Do you agree to argue for Earth?"

"I agree."

"We accept this arrangement. Present your evidence."

"Councilors, you have before you a list of crimes by the government of Tottahagan. We list the evidence in the memorandum. These are 1) the sending of agents to Earth, 2) reports sent by one of our drones detailing what happened, 3) written memo by the disruptive agent at Benton Deep Space Sensing Corporation facility in Houston, Texas in the country of the United States of America, detailing steps he took at that facility, 4) the intercepted messages sent by their agents in the country of India and in the states of Kentucky and Georgia of the United States of America to the government of Tottahagan, and 5) the agents themselves, who have made individual confessions of their crimes." Zebut again bowed deeply.

He waited, seemingly patient, as the counsel reviewed the evidence. He didn't glance at any of the Councilors, which would have been considered intrusive, but looked down as he waited.

"Prosecutor Zebut, we accept the petition to bring the verdict of guilty for crimes against the Treaty of the Year 42352. We include the provision that Tottahagan be informed of this verdict. We also feel that the representatives from Earth be able to identify the men from Tottahagan who committed the crimes. We acknowledge that Earth is a Level A-10 planet, but an exception can be made in this case. Proceed with the outline of your plan."

"Thank you, councilors." He bowed again. "Before you, you will find a Memorandum of Diplomatic Negotiation. This outlines the plan to be presented to the government of Tottahagan of the repercussions of their actions and presents a way to rectify their behavior." He bowed and stepped back, signifying he has given the floor to any who might argue for Tottahagan. No one came forward as the representative of Tottahagan to the Council of Planets had declined to attend this meeting.

"Zebut, you have done a comprehensive investigation of this matter and it is the judgement of the Council that the plan be implemented at once. As soon as the representatives identify the persons from Tottahagan as being on their planet, you can proceed with step two of your plan. Two councilors will accompany you to Tottahagan in these negotiations. We recommend Councilor Tor-Kon Aeolus and Councilor Tor-Col Soran. Are these councilors agreeable to you?"

Both named councilors stood and bowed to Zebut.

"Yes, thank you."

"We want to assure you that we have full confidence in your abilities, but this is your first experience as a prosecutor and they will be there in case you have need. Notify us as soon as the identification of these individuals have been completed. This session is concluded."

Zebut waited outside the chamber, feeling exhilarated and horrified that he was going to this strange planet. He had never been to Tottahagan. Based on reports, it seemed a dark and gloomy place, with few customs except competing for who could shout the loudest or longest. He knew that was only gossip, but he still shuttered to think about the risks involved on this trip, not only to himself and his mother, but also to the other councilor and guards. There was also the mission, his first taste of the weight of responsibility in a mission with so many factors. Thinking about the mission made him realize how much he wanted to help bring peace to two troubled worlds. But before that would happen, he had to gather the main group of people of Earth and Pebble for the identification process.

"Zebut, we will arrange for the people from Earth that you want to bring for the identification process as soon as we can, meanwhile there are a few people here to congratulate you." His mother indicated that he should look behind him.

It surprised him to see Jas, his father, striding toward him, along with his wife, Kon-Mar. Again, it doubly surprised him to receive a hug from both of them. Public shows of affection were rarely seen among their people. It delighted him. Centuries of tradition overturned in a heartbeat. Councilor Soran stepped out from his mother's office and they made bows all around. Introductions were unnecessary as his father, Commander Tor-Kon Jas and Councilor Soran had attended school together. He felt his wife's arm came around his back, and he turned to her, only to have her mouth brush by his ear. He blushed to receive a kiss in public and everyone laughed. He grinned and hugged her back.

"Come, let's celebrate your achievement and start organizing our trip," said his mother as she led the way to the councilors' private dining room.

They reviewed the procedure while they shared an excellent meal, and they exchanged best wishes for a safe and successful trip. Zebut stood staring after them as they left.

"Don't worry so much, you will see them again." Councilor Soran said. "I have been on a number of these trips, as has your mother. We will go prepared in case of trouble. We'll be all right."

"Can you describe the planet and its people for me? I wanted to study the civilization there in more detail to better understand the people, but I have only seen holograms so far, and it seems a dark and desolate place."

"Oh, it is that, all right. Their philosophy dictates that their people grow up to be hard, and seemingly greedy people. Surprisingly, a large number of their citizens don't agree with that philosophy. We try to show them another way, one that lets them live harmoniously with each other and their neighboring planets, but it is very difficult to change behavior, especially if it is the only behavior one has ever known. Like most civilizations, there are good and bad people. Right now, Tottahagan has a dictator in charge who cares little for his own people and none at all for planets that are not as advanced as his planet."

Chapter 32

"I'm really looking forward to meeting little Pebble. This small drone has certainly caused a lot of trouble," Zebut's mother, Aeolus, commented in amusement.

"I think you will be impressed with it. The bond it has formed with its Earth family is quite remarkable. I wonder how it will respond to us. I need to talk to all of them to get their co-operation to travel here and identify the Tottahagan agents."

"I'm sure they will be co-operative."

"There is a child involved. Wherever Pebble goes, Jenny goes too. Mother, wait till you see the two of them together. They are a real team."

"My, I can't wait to meet them. I will take my leave so you can work in a minute, but first I have a question for you."

"What would that be?" he asked, surprised.

"What do you think about the people of the planet Tottahagan?"

"What do you mean? The people on the planet have stolen from other planets. Aren't we helping them by showing them that there is another way?" he answered.

"Yes, it is a start, but history is full of examples of why people put up with a dictator who mistreat them. Consider that a dictator ruins or mistreats the food production, the people get desperate. Jobs disappear and people migrate to where the jobs are in order to feed their families. All I'm saying is if you want to really help this planet, think about what they need in order to change their lives."

She bowed before leaving him.

Zebut sat a long time thinking about what his mother had said.

Later, Zebut turned to his desk and waved his hand over the name of the physician he wanted to talk to about a matter that bothered him. His call was answered immediately.

The physician bowed formally to Zebut, who returned the bow, but his greeting showed the true relationship the two men had.

"Zebut, it is so good to see you," said the physician with smile.

"It's good to see you too, my friend. I have need of your experience and generosity."

"What's wrong? Are you and your wife okay? Your parents?" alarm sounding in his voice.

"Nothing is wrong with any of my family, I am sorry for alarming you. It is matter of some importance concerning one of our drones and the planet called Earth. We need to transport a number of individuals from Earth to identify some agents from Tottahagan that were stealing elements from their home world. They range in age from young to old, male and female.

My question is twofold: one, can we protect them from getting any illnesses from us, and two, can we protect us from getting any illnesses from them?"

Chapter 33

It relieved both Dan and Malinda to receive a call from Tom. It seemed like a lifetime ago that they had met Pebble and started on this adventure, but in reality, it had only been two weeks.

Dan got a wonderful welcome home from his wife. He had a huge laugh when she informed him, she had arranged a cruise for their vacation that year. When they had returned to work, the only inquiry was to Malinda hoping she had a good time on vacation. The only thought Malinda had was, I wish. The attack on Dan and Malinda when they first returned had been hushed up and dismissed because of lack of evidence and no available suspect.

Tom and Colleen looked at their wrecked house and wondered how much it would cost them to repair. Annette was not at home, so they couldn't let her know that they were home. Instead, they went on into the house and put their suitcases in the bedrooms. They expected wrecked bedrooms, but they were seemingly untouched. Colleen got busy putting things away and Tom went to check on the mail and start clearing debris. He was so busy at trying to clean up the mess that he didn't see Jenny coming down the hall to the kitchen.

"Daddy, Daddy, mommy is crying," said Jenny from the doorway. Jenny clutched Pebble in her hand as she also started to cry.

Panicked, he hurried down the hallway to their bedroom. There he found Colleen sitting on the bed, cuddling something in her hands.

"Hey, now. What's wrong?" he asked as he eased down next to her on the bed.

"Not wrong. It's okay. Annette got us a present, a present for the future." And she held up a charming set of baby clothes and matching blanket and rattle. She picked up the note that came with it. "It says, 'remember the future is always right around the corner.' Oh Tom, we have been running for what seemed like forever and I didn't even think about the baby, but Annette did." She turned into Tom's shoulder and cried.

"Will mommy be all right?" Jenny asked timidly.

Pebble looked at Jenny's worried face and did a scan of Colleen and the life she carried. "Baby and Colleen are fine, Jenny. Please don't cry."

"Oh, honey, mommy isn't crying because I'm sad." Turning, Colleen gave her daughter a huge hug.

"Yes, mommy is just happy to be home, with all of us safe and healthy, including our new baby. Come and see what Annette got the baby." Tom folded his family into his loving arms and held them close.

Chapter 34

Mary walked into the pit at Benton, feeling relief and gratitude to be home. She turned to go up to her office when she saw Henry, the director, standing a few feet away looking at her. She didn't care if it was undignified; she ran into his arms and wept. His two arms came around her and held her tight. Dimly she heard a noise and looked up into his face, which held surprise and gratefulness. She turned to see the entire staff standing at their stations and clapping their hands. Slowly, her smile blossomed on her face, and she clapped her hands for her director and all the ones who had held down the fort for them. Henry smiled and started clapping too. Later, they all had their stories to share. She was sure the stories would be told over and over for a long time and would grow bigger and more daring with each repetition. That was the way with adventures. She was just glad everyone survived.

Looking for his signal processing manager, the director scanned the room. "Where's Alex?" he asked, afraid that Alex had also been one to disappear. Embarrassed silence settled on the group. "What happened?"

Jack cleared his throat, and moved closer to the director. "Sir, I'm sorry to have to report that Alex is not here."

"What do you mean, not here?" the director asked, trying to clarify.

"No sir, what I meant to say is, he was standing right where we are now, then he just faded out, and was gone."

"I heard he threatened to blow the place up."

"Yes, sir, that part is true. He was holding a grenade, but he disappeared before he could pull the pin. We went to our science division and they came in with all kinds of meters and took readings, but couldn't figure out what happened."

He thought of the conversation with Mary about her experience with the disappearing men and his own experience in the ISMC bunker. "Well, Mary and I are thrilled to be home and we appreciate the welcome. I'm just sorry you all had to go through this experience." With that, he turned to go back up to his office. He called Harold to see if he had any disappearing workers.

"Harold, I have a question for you. Did any of your men disappear? I ask because apparently my signal processing manager was one of the men who disappeared. It seems he did a lot of damage to our systems and stations before he faded out so I need to order a complete system diagnostic to find out the extent of the damage and anything else he might have messed with.."

"We lost three people from various offices, none of the soldiers. I'm grateful that was all we lost. I have already ordered complete investigations on all the locations where we lost men.

What a mess. But we survived and without losing any of our own people. Welcome home, Henry. It's good to be back, isn't it?"

"Yes, it is and welcome home to you too. Thanks, old friend."

"Memo to Mary. Mary please order an immediate diagnostic of all systems, including wiring. Also, see that everyone gets hazard pay for the time we were gone. Thanks Mary, it's good to be back." Henry texted to Mary with a smile, knowing she would have already sent a request for a complete investigation to be done.

Soon, Mary moved down to Jack's station, receiving warm welcomes from friends and co-workers along the way. She waved and thanked everyone as she made her way down.

"I just wanted to give you and Riley a personal thank you for all your help, and I want to hear what happened here while the director and I were gone. Will you be home later tomorrow night?" Mary asked.

"Yes, we'll be home. Just a word about the others. We all worked together - it was a true team effort."

"Oh, I know, that's why I was wondering if I could impose on you one more time? Can you invite all of the people that helped with this mess and I'll cover all the costs for a thank you party? It's just that your space is a lot bigger than mine. I think it will be a big crowd. You're sure you and Riley won't mind?"

"I'm sure she would love that."

Mary wanted to get a gift for every person from the hub. This was her family away from home, but she also wanted to include her real family too. She looked up at the director's office and thought, he is like my father away from home, he and my Kentucky family kept me safe. She felt so grateful. It could have gone really badly anywhere along the way, but no one except the bad guys got hurt. Yes, she was very grateful.

Mary, Henry, Harold, Tom and his family, Annette, Dan and Malinda, and everyone from the Benton Hub, and yes, even her family from Kentucky gathered at Jack and Riley's house. Mary was overjoyed that everyone could come to this wonderful reunion of who had been together in this fight. Jenny brought Pebble and Jimmy and Mara joined them in a game of hide and seek. Pebble was surprised to meet new people, and they were equally surprised to meet the little drone. Tom and his family told the incredible story of how Pebble came to them. They also shared Zebut's name with everyone, and a toast was made in his honor.

"Look at all of us, we all survived, and maybe someday we will meet the civilization that rescued us and Pebble, as well as the amazing ambassador of that civilization," Mary said as she toasted their faraway defenders. "May we be as generous with our abilities as they were with theirs."

"I think it is enough to know that they are out there and looking after us," the director answered her with a faraway look in his eyes.

Suddenly, a shimmer started in the middle of the room. Everyone watched in fascination and fear as they saw two very tall individuals materialize. One individual carried a medical style bag and wore a long vest over his form fitting clothes. The other one was...

"ZEBUT!!" Pebble, Tom, Colleen and Jenny shouted at the same time.

Zebut smiled and bowed. As he straightened up from his bow, he deftly caught Pebble who had jumped into his hands.

"Hello, friend." Zebut looked deeply into the drone's eye.

"You came back! Jenny, look everyone, Zebut came back."

"Yes, I did and I brought a friend with me. May I introduce Physician Tor-Ninx Sano?" Physician Sano bowed to everyone and smiled. "I am so happy to meet all of you, and please call me Sano."

"Is something wrong?" Colleen pushed through the crowd.

"The Council on our planet wanted to make sure that everyone who were exposed to the agents from Tottahagan were healthy, plus I have a special request to all of you from all of us. Physician Sano and I will make sure by examining you with your permission, and Sano will take care of any medical problems. Then with your permission we will talk about the special request. Do we have your permission to examine you? Sano will examine me, so you can see." Zebut bowed deeply to the small crowd and waited patiently while everyone started to talk to each other.

Jenny came up to Zebut, and looking puzzled for a moment, bowed to him which bought a smile to both his and Sano's faces.

"Yes, Jenny, how can I help you?" Zebut asked gently, as he put Pebble back in her arms.

"My mommy is going to have a baby; can you make sure that both of them are all right?"

"Let's ask Physician Sano?" Zebut turned Jenny and Pebble toward his friend. "Jenny and Pebble have a question for you."

Physician Sano looked down at the serious face of the young child. Penny repeated her question and he thought for a moment and then said. "Can you ask your mother and father to come to me and maybe they will let me check?"

Jenny and Pebble ran to her parents and tugged on their hands until they turned to see what she wanted. Jenny started talking so fast they couldn't understand.

"Come with us to see the doctor, you too Daddy. You have to come now. Please, it's important," she kept saying as she tugged harder on her mom's hands and rushed around to push on her dad's back. Pebble contributed its voice also to Jenny's.

"Maybe you better do as they say," said Dan, who was standing nearby.

Tom and Colleen, with Jenny and Pebble's urging, moved to stand in front of the smiling physician.

"I guess we are your first guinea pigs?" Tom joked.

"Guinea pigs? What are guinea pigs?" The physician asked politely, looking around.

"I'm sorry, it was a joke. What do you want us to do?"

"Just stand there and I will scan you. It will only take a moment." He then pulled out a small tool that he moved over the length of each of them in turn. Smiling, he said, "all of you are very healthy. Colleen, your baby is growing beautifully and is free of any problems. Do you want to know the sex of the child?"

Colleen and Tom looked at each other in question, but Jenny answered with a firm YES! Tom and Colleen laughed and gave her a hug. "Yes, please."

"She is a healthy and beautiful child."

Everyone who had been listening and watching the whole procedure applauded and hugs for the new-to-be parents broke out from the crowd. Zebut's exam was not needed as people started to line up for their scans and the procedure was repeated quickly and quietly. The physician made sure that the ones with health conditions knew what they were and the ones he could fix right away, he asked to step aside. He told them he wanted to finish with the scans first and then he would talk with them about their health in more detail later. Sano worked steadily and soon everyone had been scanned and divided into groups of the ones that were perfectly healthy, ones that he could cure right away, and ones he didn't have the equipment to cure now. Some of the people were very surprised because there were a few seemingly healthy individuals who had been put in other groups.

Zebut talked quietly with various people, answering their questions, as Sano worked. When the groups were divided, Sano took out another tool and worked on the group that he could cure right away. Again, people were amazed at how quickly he could take care of a problem. These seemed to range from colds and flus to minor blood issues. He even had some people lie down on the couch and he ran the device up and down the spine to help align and take away pain. Soon, those two groups were done and he stepped back.

Zebut had waited patiently while Sano had worked. Now he addressed the whole group. He noted that everyone seemed eager to hear the rest.

"Not all of you know that our planet, Maven, has taken on the responsibility of peacekeeper in this area of space. This responsibility was asked of us by the Council of Planets and we accepted. First, we wanted to ensure that you were not harmed by the agents from Tottahagan, and second, we wanted to ensure that they were not harmed by you, like germs or other things that can be transmitted. We take this precaution because we have a request of you. The Council of Planets is bringing charges against the planet Tottahagan and we must prove that the agents we have in custody are the same individuals that were stealing and attacking you here on Earth. Would you be willing to travel to our planet and identify them?" Zebut bowed very deeply to all.

"I could identify the ones that came to our farm and would do so gladly," Amy said.

"Me too. Those men really messed up my daughter's home," Annette asserted.

Jack came forward. "I can identify a couple of the men and would be happy to do so, but a number of us could also identify the man who went by the name Alex, and maybe others that Riley and I didn't see." He looked over at the director.

"You are right, Jack. Maybe Mary and I should both go with you, and I think that Harold should go too. He had closer contact with some of them then any of us." He looked at the people he had mentioned and received a nod from all of them.

"If Tom goes, I go, and Jenny and Pebble will want to go if we go. Can we go too?" Colleen added to the chorus of assents.

"You do us great honor." Zebut and Sano both bowed to them.

Henry and Harold spoke up at the same time with a series of questions. "What method do you use to travel that distance? How far away is your planet? How long will it take to get there?"

Everyone looked at one another, wondering how do you travel in space, Movies, television, and video games were the only ideas that most people were familiar with in their lives, but everyone associated with Benton and ISMC could think of a lot of prototypes for space travel.

"The last time you saw me, I was a projection and not really on the planet. This time is a little different. We are going to teleport to our ship and then travel through hyperspace to Maven."

"So, hyperspace does exist?" asked Henry and Harold at the same time.

"Yes, indeed, it does. We couldn't be here without using it. The universe is just too large. When we travelled from the old Maven, looking for a new home, we didn't know a lot about hyperspace so we built generational ships. It took us many generations to get to our present home world. Now, we use hyperspace much more efficiently."

"What about the children?" asked Amy.

"Of course, they are coming too." That earned him a warm response from all the kids in the room. "Everyone ready?"

"What about clothes and things?"

"You won't need them because of the special property of hyperspace, you'll be back in a very short amount of time. Don't worry if you do need anything, it will be provided, after all, you are our guests."

"Okay, I guess we'll ready." Tom said as he looked around at all the nods.

"Can half the group gather around Sano?" As soon as they were gathered around the physician, Zebut gave the order and they disappeared. Nervous laughter broke out from the ones still on the planet.

"Please, gather around me and we will be on our way." They gathered around him with Jenny holding his hand and her mother's hand. Zebut gave the signal and the room disappeared from view, to be replaced by the smiling faces of their friends who were standing off to one side of the transporter pad.

"Wow, what a ride," Dan exclaimed as he looked around the interior of the ship.

Zebut smiled, "we can give you a tour of the ship in a few minutes. Please come this way." He turned and motioned for all the people to follow him. They all walked down a curving hallway that passed numerous doorways until they reached a double door. "Please go in and be comfortable." He bowed as everyone walked by him. Inside, after everyone was seated, Zebut signaled and food, desserts and drinks rose out of the table top. "Sano has already established that everything here is compatible to your taste. If you don't like anything, please let me know and I'll see that something else is served. Later, I will explain what happens next." He and Sano bowed and left the room.

Henry and Harold went around inspecting the room. They were soon joined by everyone else. The kids had fun asking the floor to make tables and chairs their size where they put their food for a picnic of their own. The rest tested areas of the walls to see what they would turn into or open. Gradually, they moved back to the tables full of food and quietly sat down.

"Colleen, it seems like a dream," Tom whispered. He looked over to Jenny and Pebble, happily playing with the other kids.

Henry and Harold came back and sat.

Jack and Riley tried a number of items on the table. "I wonder if I can get the recipe for this, that is, if we have the ingredients on Earth," she said as she put the pink and green spoonful in her mouth. Jack took a taste and agreed with her.

Zebut returned to a room unusually quiet. Everyone had tried a little of everything on the table. He smiled and bowed. "Is everyone full?" He was answered by nodding.

"Our navigation officer will be here in a short time to offer a tour of the ship and to let those interested see what travelling through hyperspace looks like. I must warn you, not everyone is comfortable looking at hyperspace." Zebut's emblem in his clothes flashed to let him know the crew member was outside the door. Zebut touched the emblem and the door pulled open.

"Officer Keano reporting." He bowed to Zebut who bowed in return and to the assembled group.

"Keano, please come and meet our guests." Zebut smiled as he invited the officer into the room. "Everyone, just say your name when you ask your questions. Keano will take very good care of you. Who wants a tour?"

Keano smiled at the enthusiasm and gathered a sizeable group and headed out the door."

Zebut turned to the remaining people. "What can I do for you?"

"I want to see hyperspace. Is that really possible? What happens if I have a reaction to it or something?" asked Henry and Harold at the same time.

Zebut looked around and noted that the children had gone with their parents and the only ones left in the room were the adults from ISMC and Benton.

"I can do that in this room. This room is located on the outer axis of the spaceship. Let me help you to prepare for your first time seeing it." He walked to the interior wall and waved his hand over a muted light in a panel which slid open. From this he took plastic-like bags that he passed around to everyone.

"I suggest you sit and face the outside wall," he said as he walked to the outside wall to stand next to another lighted panel. Before we do this, please close your eyes and when I tell you, open them slowly. The bags are there in case you experience hyperspace sickness. Ready?"

Everyone nodded and Zebut waved his hand over the light on the panel.

The panel turned transparent slowly and the group slowly opened their eyes. Some of them flinched, but most stared at the colorful streaks streaming past.

"It's so beautiful," some murmured, others just stared.

No one got sick, so Zebut made another one turn transparent. Some members of the group got up and moved closer to the window. Zebut did another one, and a few moments later, did the last one in the room. By the time Zebut turned the last one transparent everyone was at the windows staring at the beautiful display.

Zebut's emblem flashed. "I wish I could leave the panels transparent, but our other guests are done with their tour and are coming back."

Everyone reluctantly returned to their seats and Zebut made the panels return to opaque.

"Thank you, I hope everyone enjoyed their time on the ship. We will be coming out of hyperspace in a few minutes and I will open the viewing panels so you all can see my home planet." The lights in the room flashed and Zebut calmly opened the viewing panels.

Before them they could see a beautiful planet with a huge spaceport straight ahead. As they watched, the ship moved majestically toward the spaceport.

"Oh, my," moaned Annette as she sat down.

"Zebut, this is your world?" Pebble rolled over to him. "It's beautiful. I am so glad the People found such a world."

"We were only able to find it because of the efforts of thousands of drones like you. Thank you, my friend." Zebut bowed very low to the small drone. Clapping erupted from everyone behind them. Zebut picked up Pebble and turned it so it could see everyone looking at the small drone. Jenny came running up and took Pebble into her hands and gave it hug against her cheek.

"Shall we see my home?" asked Zebut and he led the way off the spaceship. Zebut bowed to the captain and crew of the ship as he ushered everyone into the space station. Physician Sano joined them as they walked down the hallway leading to the main lobby.

"I have a question for you. What do you all want to do first? Do you want the clothes I promised you or to identify the agents that attacked you?"

"Identify" came the enthusiastic response. Anger erupted on everyone's face.

"Please, follow me. We need to teleport to the surface."

"Teleport again?" The children started to dance around him, making him smile.

"Okay, follow me. Tom, Colleen and Jenny, and also, of course Pebble will step through the teleport first. Sano can follow you and then everyone can go through in groups. You will be safe, I promise."

"Zebut, can I ask you about the bowing that everyone does to everyone? Is there a custom we should know about? We don't want to offend anyone." Harold asked.

Zebut smiled at the small group that surrounded him. "Our custom of bowing has many meanings. It can represent respect, honor, love, or friendship. It can also mean greeting of a friend, or acknowledgement of an opponent. Your own world has many similar customs."

"You're right, I didn't think of other countries and their customs on our planet," said Annette, turning to Colleen and Jenny.

"That's a great idea that we can research when we get home," Colleen suggested to Jenny.

Zebut suggested that people go through the teleport single file and he stepped through.

The group looked at one another and finally Pebble jumped down, yelling to Jenny, "follow me," and rolled through the teleport, Jenny immediately followed with Colleen close behind. Tom shook his head and stepped through. The rest of the group followed quickly as if they just wanted to get it over with as quickly as possible.

Zebut hid his smile as he saw the surprised on everyone's faces. He directed the group to the side where they waited for the group with Sano to come through.

Soon, all of them were together again and chatting happily. As the group moved down the hallway and Zebut overheard comments about the colors and styles of clothes of the people they passed. Soon they arrived at another teleport, Zebut stopped so he could explain that now they would travel to the holding area of the Tottahagan prisoners.

"Will they see us or can we talk to them? I have a few things to say to a few of them," Annette said heatedly.

Others joined in with a similar opinion. Zebut listened to all of their concerns and decided to try to give them a solution.

"I promise to do what I can to accommodate all of you. Let's teleport to the detention center first and I will start enquiring about this matter. I cannot guarantee anything." Zebut bowed deeply to all.

The group followed him through the teleport to the reception area of the detention center. There they were met by the warden and a group of guards and doctors to serve as guides and answer their questions. Zebut explained to the warden the request of the people. "That request is easily accommodated. We can solve both requests, the request of the Council and the requests of the guests, at the same time. Language problems have become more frequent so we can now be solved with the use of the universal translators." At Zebut's obvious surprise at the use of universal translators, the warden mentioned that the retention center needed to use them because of the number of different people from various planets had increased the need for them.

Zebut bowed deeply to the warden, showing his vast relief that both requests could be honored.

"Could the various groups get together so you can help one another identify the men who attacked you or your group? There is one guard for each group."

As the groups formed, one guard stepped up to each group and bowed and gave his name. The guards waved the groups to follow them to various areas of the center. When they reached their areas the wall between them and the particular group of Tottahagan prisoners became transparent and they could see each other.

Zebut could hear cries of "that's him," or "hey, that's the one who fired his gun at me," or "that's the group from the ISMC bunker." As men and women were identified, they disappeared from their room to be returned to their holding cell. The identifier was then taken aside and the guard would ask questions and take statements. Everyone was surprised and pleased that they had this opportunity, and some of the prisoners also responded that they were sorry. Mostly the leaders from the Tottahagan group were still hostile.

"Thank you so much for this," Tom and his family told Zebut. "It felt good to be able to tell them how their actions affected us. Some even apologized."

Others expressed the same reaction. Annette had the longest conversation with her group of attackers, with typical results of the leader not being sorry and the others expressing sorrow for breaking the door and wrecking the kitchen of her daughter and son-in-law's house. The guards assured the various groups that their statements would be very effective toward the prisoners' futures, especially the leaders who were not sorry.

Henry, Mary and Harold were very upset with the leader "Alex." He had not only held Henry against his will, but had also threatened to murder everyone at the Benton in Houston. Alex refused to speak to them, but they were very happy to make statements against him. All the men and women of Benton gleefully signed statements against him.

Zebut assured all of the Earth inhabitants that he would have the statements delivered to the Council.

"Meanwhile, I have a treat for all of you. We can walk there if you want or we can teleport."

"I would like to walk and see some of the sights of your world," declared Annette. Most of the people agreed with her so the group set off with Zebut acting as guide and answering all their questions. Sano joined them when they reached the store.

"My friends, our gift to you is in this store. Please, follow me." Zebut was flooded by many questions, especially from all the children. Sano smiled as he watched Zebut deal with so many at once. Sano knew Zebut had had little interaction with children, but Zebut seemed to be really enjoying talking to each one.

"Zebut, one moment please."

Zebut stopped surprised to hear his mother's voice behind him. He turned quickly and bowed deeply. When he straightened from his bow, he was doubly surprised to see, not only his mother, but his father and wife too. Again, he bowed and wondered why his family had come together like this. He was startled by the open show of affection when his wife stepped to him and gave him a kiss on the cheek. He could feel a blush rising up his neck and he laughed at himself and his family joined in on his self-depreciation. Sano clapped his shoulder and turned back to the curious members of the group. Zebut enjoyed introducing all the visitors from Earth.

"Zebut, may I borrow some of your new friends?" his mother, Aeolus asked. "I specifically need Tom, Colleen, Jenny and Pebble."

"Of course," he said as he wondered what was so urgent that his family was here, and why his mother wished to speak to his friends.

"My friends," he said to the group, "Tom, Colleen, Jenny and Pebble, my mother wishes to speak with you."

"Let us go in the store, and I'll talk while we shop." And she led the way into the store. "I know Zebut wants to give you some of our style of clothing. So here we are and I think Zebut has already talked with the sales people. If you have any questions, I'm here to help." She turned to the sales specialist who immediately stepped forward. Aeolus watched as each one was introduced to the visualizer. As she suspected, Colleen and Jenny were the most enchanted by the new-to-them way of trying on clothes. She took advantage of talking to them privately when they finished making their choices.

She bowed deeply and said to them, "The Council of Planets has requested that you stay a little longer than the others because we need your services a little longer."

"Of course, we would be happy to help, but can you tell us why?" Colleen asked.

"Yes, indeed, I can. Your help with identifying the prisoners was very helpful. The Council thinks that if Pebble goes with the prosecutor to present the negotiation, then Earth would be represented. They chose Pebble as Earth's ambassador because the reports it sent were responsible for us becoming aware of what the planet Tottahagan was stealing from Earth."

"Who is the prosecutor?" asked Tom.

"I am very proud to say that Zebut has been chosen."

"Pebble, you get to go with Zebut to another planet! That's so exciting," exclaimed Jenny.

Tom asked Aeolus, "is it dangerous?"

She smiled at Pebble, "Pebble can protect Zebut, but even though this has an element of danger to it, it really shouldn't be dangerous for us. The other councilor and I will be there too and we will have guards. We shouldn't be gone too long. We, of course, will see to your comfort while we are gone."

"Are all of us staying?" Tom inquired as he looked around at the group standing with Zebut, some of which were still choosing their new clothes.

"No, the Council thought the rest of the group could be returned to Earth. Only you and your family would stay the extra time. Would that be acceptable to you? Or would you like the whole group to stay? That could also be arranged."

"Could they decide for themselves? Some might have reasons they need to return to Earth."

"Of course, we will ask them if they want to stay. We could also arrange some fun things for the children to do," Aeolus told him. "Meanwhile, please come with me for a special surprise." She led the way to a special area of the store where necklace designs were made from gold.

"Wow, these are so beautiful," admired Colleen.

"Is that real gold?" exclaimed Tom.

"Yes, Pebble must look the part also." She led the way to the back where there were seats and invited them to sit down. After everyone is seated, she gave the okay to the artist, who began to lie out the beautiful open-top basket on a velvet cloth. The little basket was a little more than a half basket where Pebble could sit and see everything but f Pebble needed to get out of the basket it could also jump out.

Jenny thought it didn't look like an Easter basket, but kind of like a baby swing. "Look Pebble, you can jump out if you want!"

"Pebble, this is to be worn around the Zebut's neck and one will be fashioned for Jenny as well. The material is pure gold and the artist will adjust it to fit properly. You are now the Earth Ambassador and will accompany us to Tottahagan for the negotiations. Tom, do you mind standing in for Zebut to try it on? He doesn't know about the necklace. I want it to be a surprise."

Tom gingerly picked up the necklace and put it over his head. Aeolus turned to Jenny and asked her to put Pebble in the basket. The artist immediately bent to adjust the basket so Pebble was not restricted, but also would not fall out. Pebble looked the basket over and looked at the artist and said, "it is so smooth." The startled artist jumped.

"Sorry, I didn't mean to startle you," Pebble said politely, which had the artist backing away and bowing deeply.

"Oh my, I should have introduced Pebble to you. It is a very important drone. Pebble, this is the famous artist, Bobrun. Bobrun, this is Ambassador Pebble of the Planet Earth."

"My apologies, Ambassador." Turning to Aeolus he said, "Councilor, the other necklace will be adjusted right away and both will be sent to your home as you requested."

Bowing deeply, she said, "thank you for your wonderful work, the Council are very grateful."

Quickly, they returned to the main group. Zebut had gathered them all together in a lovely setting of a fountain and grove of fruit trees. There he had bags filled with another surprise.

Smiling, he said, "this one is from me. It has been a pleasure to meet each of you. I hope this will remind you of your time with us here on Maven." And he bowed very deeply, as helpers passed his gifts out to all his guests.

At first, they seemed puzzled, but helpers pressed the hidden button on the bottom and a wonderful hologram spring up showing a 3-dimentionial picture of everyone in their group, plus a picture of Zebut and Pebble.

"Oh, this is wonderful, but when did you take photographs of all us. Thank you so much, now I'll have something to remember all of you," said Annette, as she broke down into tears. Jenny and Colleen immediately wrapped her in their arms. Others also came forward to comfort her.

Zebut also came forward, and tentatively reached out for her hand. She also reached out. "I also will miss all of you, but I have been told that my mother and I must leave at once. We will see you soon. Goodbye for now." And he turned away to his wife and his mother and walked briskly with them to the nearest teleport and was gone.

Zebut's father, Tor Kon Ninx and his friend, Sano explained that Zebut had the photographs taken as everyone went through the first teleport. They then helped everyone get to their rooms so they could rest and wait. Excited, they had a great time trying on clothes and marveling at the hologram cube. Ninx and Sano had a good time with the lively crowd. and by the time they left they agreed with Zebut that Humankind were a mix of delightful and insightful people and could see why Zebut liked them so much.

Chapter 35

"Come, let's get aboard our ship. All of your materials are waiting for you with copies for the officials on Tottahagan. The prisoners are on board too," Aeolus told him. "I know you have already studied the procedures we will follow."

Zebut followed the councilors onto the ship and took his customary seat. "Don't sit there, my son. Today, you are the prosecutor and, as such, sit in a place of honor. Sit here instead." She indicated the middle seat behind the pilots while she and Soran took the seats flanking him with the guards seated behind them.

The councilors were silent, so he could form his own impressions during the trip. He had always loved space travel because of the beauty of the universe. His first thought when they approached Tottahagan was dismay. Grey to black clouds bellowed in the atmosphere. Descending through the dirty-looking clouds, he saw tall smoke stacks belching out even more oily black smoke, adding to the grimy look of the buildings surrounding the spaceport. Everything had a grey look to it. *How can they breathe?* he wondered. When they touched down, he saw workers who had such heavy burdens that they were bent double as they scurried to do their tasks.

"Come, we need to prepare ourselves for our confrontation with the officials."

They headed back to private rooms to dress in their ornamental robes. Zebut had seen his mother in her ceremonial robes, but this was his first time donning the ornate gold embroidered robes himself. He marveled at the feel of the beautiful material and the heavy weight.

"Zebut, this is for your protection, please wear it." Aeolus placed a small woven gold necklace around his neck. It had a half-basket of honor on his overcoat. Into this basket she placed Pebble. She also pined a protection brooch on his sash under the necklace. "Don't worry, both Soran and I will also wear these brooches. It's a prototype, but if anyone attacks us, it should repel any type of weapon with equal force. Both you and Pebble should be protected. Very practical if it works."

"The prisoners will stay on the ship under guard while the negotiations are going on inside," Soran informed him. "We do have a regiment of soldiers with us as part of our honor guard, but they can provide protection too."

"Remember, head up and shoulders back. You are the Prosecutor, the ultimate judge and jury for these crimes and as such, you deserve honor," his mother told him.

Zebut looked down at Pebble and whispered, "we are in this together, old friend. Thank you for coming."

Pebble told him in simple terms, "I need to protect you."

Zebut was surprised by the simple statement, but it made him feel very close to the little drone that was the start of this whole matter. He thought to himself, it was right and just that the drone be in at the end of this matter.

A runner came to tell them that the government officials were ready to receive them. Zebut would have moved out, but Soran stopped him.

"We are the representatives of the Council of Planets and the Prosecutor from the planet Maven here on official business. We will wait here until an appropriate representative party comes to welcome us onto your planet."

"But… but what do I say to them?" the runner asked nervously.

"Tell them what I said," Soran answered.

Minutes later, a solemn group approached. One stepped forward.

"Please, Councilors, be welcome to our humble planet. Honored Prosecutor, be welcome." He bowed and waited for a response.

"I notice you do not state your name or rank. Please do so now," Soran demanded. Zebut noticed the runner from earlier was behind him, and now had a vivid bruise on his cheek. The man stammered his name and rank.

"So, they send a minor official now. Send your ranking official or we will decide you are not interested in negotiations and so wish to revoke the treaty. We demand the official welcome of a Prosecutor."

The man and his entourage practically ran from the ship.

"That's how it's done. Watch and learn," his mother murmured to Zebut.

Zebut looked around at the condition of the people working on the landing site. They were sick looking and as he watched he saw a bent man steal a lunch from a nearby bench. Why the people doing the hard work are starving, like mother was telling me, he thought with sudden insight.

"I'll be right back," he whispered to his mother as he stepped back to talk quietly with the captain of their ship.

Aha, now we are getting somewhere," Soran said to Zebut when he rejoined the councilors.

A large procession came up the lane before the ship. A group of dignitaries followed a group of extravagantly dressed men and women who moved to both sides. The dignitaries came forward and offered brief bows.

While the group from Maven waited Soran glanced over at Zebut. Zebut was whispering to Pebble who said yes in answer. Soran wondered what was said between them, but the Tottahagan delegation had arrived and he turned his attention to meet them.

"My name is Boratti and I am the Chief Official of the Tottahagan Government. Welcome to our humble planet. We are honored to have the prosecutor here to discuss the treaty," he said with a slight bow.

The Councilors all gave an equal bow in response and stepped forward to follow the officials. The Tottahagan guards that surrounded them made Zebut a little nervous, because though they might be lavishly dressed, he caught the sight of knives and guns as they moved. He followed his mother's guidance and kept his head high and shoulders back, even though he had an itch between his shoulder blades, but he noted the people standing on either side of their procession had no weapons. His first impression was one of dismay for the squalor of the shops and homes they passed, and the people they passed kept their eyes down. His second impression was sadness that the people were treated so badly. The Hall of the People was the biggest granite building in a large central plaza. Its towers dominated the small shops and homes that ringed the plaza. The dingy stonework showed the ancient age of the building with its carved frescoes and intricate designs covering the entire front. It would have been beautiful when it was new. They moved into the Hall of the People which immediately struck Zebut as being unused. The soaring beams were beautiful, but everything looked unclean, everything except the huge golden chair facing the crowd. After the chief official sat in the golden throne, he invited them to sit in places of honor on a central dais. The rest of the Tottahagan party took seats surrounding the dais and citizens filled every available space inside the immense hall. The itch between Zebut shoulder blades increased. He noted that the guards took up positions surrounding the dais, behind the dignitaries. In turn, they were backed by the guards for Zebut and his party. His mother stood and spoke in a clear voice that carried up to the rafters.

"I am Councilor Tor-Kor Aeolus and this is Councilor Soran. We accompany Prime Prosecutor Zebut. We are here to negotiate crimes committed by citizens of the planet Tottahagan. You have received notice of these crimes. How say you?"

"Councilor, yes we received them, but we deny these crimes," Boratti answered in a thundering voice, jumping to his feet.

She sat down when Boratti sat and Zebut stood in the center facing the Chief Administrator Boratti. The people waited eagerly to hear what he had to say.

"I am Zebut of the planet Maven, and am the Prime Prosecutor in this matter as appointed by the Council of Planets. Before you, you will find a Memorandum of Diplomatic Negotiation, detailing the crimes and the names of the citizens of Tottahagan who committed them." Zebut watched the other officials for their reactions. He saw resignation, but also anger directed toward Boratti.

Boratti again jumped from his seat and shouted, "I said we deny these crimes!"

"Do you deny that these individuals are citizens of the planet?" Zebut asked him calmly.

"Yes, we do deny them! How dare you question my word." Boratti shouted, getting red in the face.

The officials that were sitting with the chief official and most of the audience murmured in dismay.

"They claim citizenship to Tottahagan. Do you have confirmation that they are not legal citizens?" Zebut demanded.

"Chief Official, I recognized some of these names. You cannot deny them their citizenship," the official on his right asserted. Members of the audience and some other officials nodded their heads in agreement.

Boratti glared at him and hissed, "be silent! You know nothing."

Zebut looked at the other officials around Boratti and decided to play the message that showed Boratti to be a liar.

"Please play the intercepted message sent from the planet Earth to planet Tottahagan on the thirteen day of the month of Bur, year 42405."

The officials sat stunned as they listened to the message. All recognized the voice of the official talking to the agent on planet Earth. Chief Official Boratti sat in powerless rage. Slowly, one by one, the officials turned their backs on him. Members of the audience hissed at him and yelled for his removal from office. He slowly stood up, turning his rage on Zebut.

"You have no right to dictate to us. That planet deserved to be used by us. You did this to me. You are an interfering fool and you will pay," Boratti stood braced and hissed in a threatening matter.

Before Zebut realized his danger, the chief official whipped out a throwing knife. Pebble saw the knife as it was pulled out and flashed a piercing bright light just as Boratti threw the blade. The brilliant light jarred Boratti's aim and the brooch slowed the dagger, but did not totally deflect the knife. It passed through the protective shell of the brooch and embedded itself in Zebut's shoulder, causing him to stumble back and down the steps. The look of triumph only lasted a few seconds as the brooch hit Boratti with a force beam and other multiple beams from various weapons of nearby officials and the Maven guards. He was dead before his body crashed to the floor. The Maven guards immediately surrounded the fallen prosecutor and councilors, facing off against the Tottahagan guards.

His mother was the first to reach Zebut, with Soran a close second.

Zebut called out "Pebble?" His hand felt around him for Pebble. "Is Pebble okay?"

"Stay still," Aeolus told her son as he tried to rise. "We must get back to the ship," She said to Soran. Zebut was vaguely aware of what was going on around him but couldn't seem to move. Finally, everything faded away.

Pebble, who had fallen out of the open-top basket when Zebut had stumbled backwards, rolled over to Soran and jumped into his hands who held it tight and put it back in the basket on the chain around Zebut's neck.

Panic reigned in the hall. Officials stood unsure of what to do, and the few Maven soldiers with them moved closer to better protect their official party. No one threatened the party from Maven.

"Masters, let us help him. We pledge to take good care of the young master. Please come with us," a group of men and women pleaded as they came forward and gently lifted Zebut and carried him to a nearby house that was located right beside the hall. There they laid him on a bed and tried to remove his clothes so they could reach the wound.

"Good mother, can you remove the protection brooch and chain so we can get to the knife?" the leader, a woman, asked of

Aeolus, who gently removed the brooch and moved the chain with Pebble to the side so the healer could work.

"Soran, call the ship and advise them of what has happened and our location. I will remain here and help tend to Zebut. Can you proceed with the negotiations?"

"Of course, right away." He hurried away to call the ship and went back across the plaza and into the hall again to renew the negotiations that had been interrupted.

Soran soon finished the initial negotiations and turned over the prisoners to the new Chief Official. He made sure that the agreement was written and duplicated for both parties. Zebut could finish the more detailed negotiations when he recovered. He thought once the prisoners saw the blood on the steps, they would change their ways, but that could be hopeful wishing on his part. The new chief official's name was Vrabel and seemed to be a more moderate man.

"Boratti was a tyrant and dealt with the population as slaves. He bullied his way into power and he got what he deserved in the end" he said without a glance at the corpse. "Don't worry, master, the woman is one of our best healers. Healer Alyxandra will take excellent care of the prosecutor." He had noted the worried glances Soran and the guards were casting toward the healer's house.

"Thank you for your help," Soran said. "We would not want this to lead to war between our planets."

"No, no, indeed not," he said as he brought his mind back to the reason for their visit.

"Chief Official, I know that the prosecutor had a list of possible programs to help your people deal with the pollution and other problems your planet is suffering from, if you care to take advantage of his generosity."

"The Prosecutor is most kind. I would be delighted to look at them. Maybe we can come to an understanding."

"Oh, I think you will appreciate hearing the clever way he thought to use the returning prisoners in the new growth of your economy."

"Use the prisoners, have them earn their keep and learn a new skill at the same time, so to speak? Yes, brilliant. I will enjoy reading all his recommendations. Please excuse me, I need to speak to the other officials," he said as he bowed and backed away.

The ship's captain called Soran to inquire about Zebut's condition just as Soran walked out of the hall. "Sir, our ship's medical officer should be there soon and will help in his care."

"Thank you, Captain, send a detail to help transport Zebut back to the ship." Soran realized that he had heard no reports from Aeolus in a considerable amount of time. Just as he thought he might check on Zebut and Aeolus, they came out of the house. Zebut had his arm strapped up and he was a little unsteady on his feet, but he was up and moving, albeit slowly. Walking beside him were his mother and the healer, deep in conversation.

"Soran, we must invite Healer Alyxandra to Maven. She does amazing things. Just look at Zebut, he's practically healed."

Zebut's head turned toward Soran when he heard his mother speak Soran's name.

"Soran, I'm so glad you are okay. It seems that Pebble and the brooch helped deflect and slow the blade, so the damage is not bad. It just hurts a little and my head feels strange," Zebut said as he carefully walked to him. Soran grabbed his good arm when Zebut staggered a little.

"I think we should talk to the manufacturers of the brooches, I thought they would stop everything. Apparently, that's not true. Congratulations on being the first subject to try them." Soran teased him as he led him to a seat on a garden wall in front of the Hall.

"Thanks for that information," Zebut gave him a half laugh in response. He looked down at Pebble, "thanks for my life." Pebble purred back at him. "Wait, I need to tell the new leader that there are ships coming with food and emergency supplies for the people who need them. I need to tell someone. . tell my mother I see what she was trying to help me understand," he murmured as he could feel himself start to fade out.

The detail from the ship arrived with an antigravity stretcher and the ship's medical officer who went to confer with the healer. It was an easy matter to ease Zebut down on the stretcher. Zebut protested that he could walk back to the ship, but his protests died as he laid down flat. It only took a minute and he was asleep. Soran knew that when they got back to the ship, the physician would run a complete scan, just in case. Pebble was still in the basket, so Soran knew Zebut was in very good hands. Soran bowed to Pebble in thankfulness.

Soran smiled because of Zebut's spirit and Pebble's bravery. Zebut and Pebble had worked as a real team. They will go down in history as the Heroes of the Great Tottahagan's Change. He was sure it would make young Zebut blush and Pebble very happy for his friend.

THE END
OR IS IT?

Epilogue

Eight months later:

Tom, Colleen, Jenny and Pebble welcomed their newest addition to the family just in time for Christmas. They named her "Grace." Pebble was especially excited to see such a small version of Jenny. It took lots of recordings. These it sent to its new friend, Drone.

Two days after arriving home, Colleen found the painting she had done of Jenny and Pebble sleeping. She didn't remember that she had rolled it up and put it in the closet. She and Tom were very grateful that the men that had made their lives so miserable had not found it. They would have probably destroyed it. It was fun for Jenny and Pebble to help Colleen to mat and frame it, and Tom hung the painting in Jenny's room. Colleen now had plans to do a family portrait with Tom, herself, Jenny, Grace and Pebble.

The People's Drone, as they called it, always wondered what it would be like to be on the surface of a planet. Because it had such a big part in helping Pebble, it kept asking questions that

Pebble was only too glad to answer. Unbeknown by anyone else, they still remained in touch, sharing what they could and learning from each other.

Dr. Malinda Gold continued in her job as a geologist at Dianna Research in Columbus, but was now dating a very handsome biologist who worked in the same building as Dan. He was one of her rescuers from the unknown assailant. Now she doesn't come home to just a cat.

Dr. Dan Cooper continued to work, but now dreams of sailing the ocean blue with his wife of 49 years. He caught the bug when he came home from his adventures with Pebble. His wife gave him a gift of a cruise and he fell in love with the sea. He is already planning their next cruise, a birthday present for his wife. If you visit him, be careful, because he cherishes time to pull out his picture albums to share. They are beautiful, but there are a lot of them.

Dr. Henry Evans, also known as the Director of Benton Deep Space Sensing Corporation, is now content to stay home and play with his grandkids. He decided he missed companionship, so he joined a few clubs and takes one of his grandchildren at a time out on what he calls "special days with Grandpa." He keeps up with news about Benton and all his many friends there. It thrilled him when Mary got promoted as the new director. He knew that with her quick mind and background she'd do an excellent job.

When Mary Matthews isn't busy with her new role, she makes more time to visit her family in Wyoming and in Kentucky. She has her eye on a special someone, but she won't name him to anyone. Jimmy and Mara are delighted with visiting their aunt Mary. She and her cousin Davy take Mara and Jimmy horseback riding, and Christine enjoys challenging Mary on target practice.

It surprised Jack and Riley to find their family grow. Mary's family showed up at their door one day with a delightful little terrier mix they found on their farm. As Nick explained it, "it's so little, something will try to eat it, so it'll be safer here. So here. No thanks are necessary." Jack and Riley are still trying to get over their shock, but the first time the puppy licked their noses, they were hooked.

Last, but not least, the people on Earth were unaware of the aftershocks of their close call with Tottahagan, but Zebut wasn't. He is still reeling from everyone treating him as a hero. He just wanted to go back to his work with no fanfare, but that doesn't seem to be something that will happen soon. He talked with his father, who told him to just relax and enjoy the moment because it won't last forever. He can't wait for the next emergency to happen to someone else, so he can stop blushing. Besides, Soran just smirks when someone calls him a hero.

Oh, did I remember to tell you that the People's Drone and Pebble liked to gossip? Well, you knew, right? They may be the first unrecognized first contact ever for the people of Earth. Who knows what they could cook up? After all, the People gave them artificial intelligence. Maybe we should monitor the heavens, just in case. Those drones are a slippery sort, always looking into things and reporting back to one another. Who knows what they think about humans? I mean, Pebble loves its family, but who knows what the People's Drone thinks. Another thing to think about is that there are hundreds of People's Drones out there in space, just sailing around with not much to do but spy on planets. What if they decide that Earth is the perfect place to park for a while? What would we do if that happened? I suggest that we teach them all about baseball, basketball, football, painting, fused glass, stained glass, jewelry making, model railroad making, and all the other kinds of making things. Let alone computers, medical technology, and machine engineering. In other words, we should teach them everything about us, our dreams, our wishes for our future or even our search for life away from our planet. We could share the excitement of exploring our solar system. Maybe the People would rethink how grown up we are and give us another chance. They may be the best friend a planet ever had.

Well, this is really the end.

I think.

THE END

IN APPRECIATION

I want to say thank you to my wonderful family, for all of their support and encouragement during the writing of this story.

My husband Richard
Daughter - Malinda
Son – Nicholas and his wife Amy
Grandchildren – Riley, Davy, and Mara

Alpha Readers:
Malinda Mowrey, Nancy Carney, Connie Jenkins,
Jim Saylor, and Jessica Armstrong

Beta Readers:
Malinda Mowrey and Connie Jenkins

Copy Editor: Heidee Howard

And a huge Thank You to everyone at the following for their
expertise and guidance:

IngramSpark
ProWritingAid
SelfPubBookCovers
Integrative Ink